'Raif,' she murmured longingly, as his hands moved her clothing, exposing her rounded breasts to his caressing touch.

'Karen, no. . . That's more than enough.'

Before she had time to take in the stiffening of his arm muscles, Raif had pushed himself away from her, leaving her vulnerable and chilled as cool air touched her tender skin. Quickly she clutched the gaping sides of her blouse together with shaking hands.

'I'm sorry,' he was saying, staring at the floor and breathing heavily.

'Why? I don't understand. . .' she began, hearing the high note of pain in her own voice.

'This can't go on. I shouldn't have asked you here tonight. I might have known. . .'

'But why?' she repeated, not caring, yet, how desperate it sounded.

Lilian Darcy is Australian, but has recently married and now makes her home in New Jersey. She writes for theatre, film and television as well as her romance fiction work, and her interests include winter sports, music, travel and the study of languages. Hospital volunteer work and friends in the medical profession provide the research background for her novels, which she enjoys writing because of the opportunity they give for creating realistic, modern stories, believable characters and a romance that will stand the test of time.

Previous Titles

SISTER PAGE'S PAST
CALLING AIR DOCTOR THREE
VALENTINES FOR NURSE CLEO

UNWILLING PARTNERS

BY

LILIAN DARCY

MILLS & BOON LIMITED
ETON HOUSE   18–24 PARADISE ROAD
RICHMOND   SURREY   TW9 1SR

All the characters in this book have no existence outside the imagination of the Author, and have no relation whatsoever to anyone bearing the same name or names. They are not even distantly inspired by any individual known or unknown to the Author, and all the incidents are pure invention.

All Rights Reserved. The text of this publication or any part thereof may not be reproduced or transmitted in any form or by any means, electronic or mechanical, including photocopying, recording, storage in an information retrieval system, or otherwise, without the written permission of the publisher.

MILLS & BOON and Rose Device is registered in U.S. Patent and Trademark Office.

First published in Great Britain 1990 by Mills & Boon Limited

© Lilian Darcy 1990

Australian copyright 1990

ISBN 0 263 12723 0

Set in 10 on 11 pt Linotron Plantin
15-9010-58417
Typeset in Great Britain by Centracet, Cambridge
Made and printed in Great Britain

CHAPTER ONE

THERE hadn't been a spring this wild for years. The old-timers had been saying it for over a week now, and it was still only the second week in May. Tonight was the wildest, though. Early summer visitors had battened the windows and doors of their holiday cottages, and transient tourists had decided they'd have to miss the sight of Mount St Helens in favour of heading south tomorrow towards the more reliable warmth of Oregon and California. Locals had just listened to the forecasts, shaken their heads, and carried on as usual.

It was just after nine when the news about the cruise ship had come. They said nearly two thousand vessels had been wrecked off this coast, where the wide torrent of mountain water that poured from the mouth of the Columbia River mingled with the snaking currents of the Pacific Ocean. Shipwrecks were much rarer now, of course. The powerful beams from lighthouses at Cape Disappointment and North Head could be seen for miles as they swathed out to sea.

'There's a cruise ship gone aground off the Cape, Raif.' Will Thomas's phone call had cut across a solitary evening of classical music on the compact disc player and the crackling companionship of an open fire.

Now, just on two hours later, the warmth and peace of that fire was no more than a memory. Dr Raiford Calvert had doused it thoroughly last thing before leaving the house. On a night like this, a draught. . .sparks blown on to the rectangle of woollen rug that covered the wooden floor. . . Coming home to a charred wreck instead of his beloved house? No, thank you!

He shivered as he thought of the luxurious heat of that fire, though. He was already drenched to the bone in spite of full storm gear and two thick pullovers beneath. The coastguard boat plunged on through the surging waves and into the rain-lashed darkness. Raif looked across at Will Thomas. The bridge of his nose was blue with cold and his jaw was clenched to keep shivering under control. At the moment, they were both standing in the shelter of the boat's cabin, but it was their second trip out to the doomed *Star of Scandinavia*, and, on the first journey, the work of rescue and emergency medical aid had given them no opportunity to think of shelter.

'You shouldn't have come, Will,' Raif said, but the older doctor shook off the words with an irritated shrug.

'Stop nursemaiding!' he said. 'I was needed. I've been doing this for years.'

'Come on. . . How long since a ship of this size went down?' Raif challenged.

Jim Teague, the man at the controls of the vessel, turned around at this question. 'Not since I came here, and that's fifteen years ago,' he said.

'Well, I've been here thirty-eight,' Dr Thomas barked.

There was a small silence, and Raiford Calvert exchanged a quick glance with Jim Teague. There came a time when experience had to take second place to the strength and fitness of youth. Raif was afraid that Will Thomas had reached that critical time, and an added undercurrent to his concern about the safety of the fourteen hundred passengers aboard the *Star of Scandinavia* was his fear that tonight's consequences for Will would be more than just a bad cold in the head.

He thought of the conversation they had had several hours ago when Will had dropped into Raif's surgery after seeing the last patient in his own.

'Had a funny call this morning,' he had said. 'A woman. Wanted to know if the practice was for sale.'

'And what did you tell her?' Raif had asked, although he had known what the answer would be.

'I told her it was going to you, either gradually over the next couple of years as I pass patients on to you, or all at once, if I don't last that long.'

'Don't say that!' Raif had answered sharply. The older man had been a good friend and a good doctor. He deserved to enjoy years of peaceful retirement.

'Still,' Dr Thomas had said, 'I'd better make that will. Get it all in writing.'

'I wonder who the woman was. . .'

'And how she'd heard a rumour about the practice.'

'Did you get her name?' Raif had asked.

'No. I started to ask, but she'd already hung up. It was long-distance.'

No time to think any more about that conversation now. The coastguard vessel was within sight of the crippled vessel by this time. Raif heard Jim Teague's sharp intake of breath. 'Look at the angle of lean on her now,' he said.

The second crew member clicked his tongue and Raif studied the ship, peering through the stinging rain and icy, windy darkness. Yes, no doubt about it. The lean was much more pronounced. He was no mariner. Jim Teague and Russell Blaski had theorised about the disaster—an engine explosion that had holed the hull, a drastic mistake in navigation, entrapment by the shifting sand bar beyond the mouth of the great river—but no one as yet really knew what had happened, or what would happen next. Clearly, though, the vessel's lean was not a good sign.

Stick to what you know, Raif told himself sternly. Medical assistance. Other coastguard boats were hard at work shepherding the passenger-filled lifeboats safely to shore. Other rescue workers were already beginning the agonising process of trying to account for all souls aboard the ship. If it became too dangerous to approach the *Star of Scandinavia*, they would be informed by radio, or Jim Teague would make a decision about it himself.

From what Raif could judge, the launch of lifeboats and rescue of crew and passengers had been calm and orderly so far. On their previous trip out to the vessel, they'd only had to deal with three casualties, and those three would already be in hospital by now.

A blurred white shape loomed towards them in the darkness, one of the vessel's sturdy lifeboats.

'Too many—look at them,' Jim Teague said.

Raif had seen it at that moment too. Twice as many bodies as the boat was designed to hold huddled against the wind, and the pale, tossing sides were dangerously low in the water.

'We'll pick some of them up, and alert *Chinook Three*,' Jim Teague said, referring to another coastguard boat. 'Something's happened.'

Within a few minutes, they knew what it was. The first soaking, shivering man to be pulled aboard stumbled out an explanation through chattering teeth.

'They can't launch the boats,' he told them. 'The ship's leaning too far. The cables and pulleys won't swing, and I d-don't know what. . . People are jumping.'

'Jumping? This water's deathly cold!' Jim said.

'They're frightened,' said the man.

'How many?' Raif demanded.

'I don't know. Fifty more? Most of the boats were launched. The last ones are staying behind like we did to pick up the extras, but people'll get lost. They'll drown. . .My wife. . .' He couldn't go on.

Within five minutes, ten people from the overloaded boat had been brought safely on to the deck. *Chinook Two* was moving again, and the lifeboat itself was making its way towards the shore, where one of the other coastguard vessels would take it under her wing.

These people needed medical treatment, weakened as they were by their long wait to be lauched in a boat, and they risked hypothermia. *Chinook Two* was well equipped for the work, but it took all Raiford Calvert's attention. When the quality of the boat's engine sound changed and he looked up, he expected to see the coastguard wharf hoving into view, with its dramatic pulses of light from ambulances and search beams.

Instead, he saw greyness, and took a moment to realise what it was—the great pale side of the *Star of Scandinavia* towered over them, leaning like some coastal cliff at a terrifying angle.

'I don't like this. . . I don't like this,' Jim Teague was saying.

The ten rescued passengers were silent—some with fear, Raif guessed, other with the numbness of shock.

'But I've got to see if there's anyone still in the water. . .' Jim continued.

He was handling the boat as if it were a rodeo horse, now idling, now revving, steering as close to the side of the stricken ship as he dared, and then away again, as a surge in the dangerous storm waves threatened to pound the two vessels—one giant, one seemingly tiny—against one another.

Raif stared out at the waves. He had received another drenching as he and Will helped to pull the lifeboat passengers aboard, but he'd stopped even thinking of his own body now. The waves were a dancing blur of rain-lashed shapes, a feverish hallucination of movement and form. White foam tricked itself into the shape of a face or an arm, a momentary swell could have been a shoulder, and there was debris in the water now too. People had tried to bring possessions, and had then abandoned them to the sea.

Jim had radioed to another coastguard boat with the news about the failed launchings, and it should arrive soon to help ease the load on the crowded lifeboats, which were still dangerously close to the ship. *Chinook Two* was closest of all, and the hope of them finding anyone still alive in this water was diminishing by the minute. They chugged in a lurching sweep along the side of the vessel.

'Is that angle of lean getting worse?' Jim began.

'I think so,' Russell Blaski said quietly.

'We can't stay any longer,' Jim muttered.

Then Raif saw something—or he thought he did. A white shoulder. A blonde head. Two heads. Two people still alive out there? Or just debris from the deck, perhaps a piece of empty clothing?

'It *is* someone!' he said.

'Yes!' Jim had glimpsed the uncertain shapes now too. He fought with the boat. 'Thank God they're a good distance from the ship.'

'A good distance?' Russell said tightly.

'Further than we are.'

The two figures disappeared from sight, then were seen again much closer.

'Raif. . .' Will Thomas gestured to where Russell Blaski was lowering a ladder down the side of the boat. Raiford nodded.

Will's face was creased with cold and exhaustion. He was still binding an arm that had been gashed by the wild swing of a pulley as the lifeboat was launched. Raif stood ready on the outside deck of the boat. Will could stay inside. The two heads were almost alongside now. A wave rose and the heads were submerged.

Russell muttered under his breath, 'One's only a kid!'

'I can't hold up. . .' It was the kid, a girl, in her teens, and the voice was a moan of exhaustion. She had been gripping the other, paler body, and now let go and sank almost out of sight. With a quick oath, Russell Blaski tore off the thick yellow storm jacket he wore and dived in. Raif was only a moment behind.

The water was an insult to every nerve in his system—cold, black, wild, stinging with salt. For a moment he lost control and flailed helplessly, limbs refusing to respond, then he surfaced, feeling the muscles of his head shrink against the bone of his skull like a vice. The kid—the girl—was already in Russell's arms. But where was the larger, paler body, the white shoulders he had seen. . .?

There! He saw a shape, already several yards away and separated from him by a mountain of wave. She—was it a she? He thought so—was going under. He lunged through the water, dived down, gripped and pulled. He had her.

He manoeuvred until he was floating on his back, supporting her along his whole length with her legs trailing inertly between his own as he frog-kicked powerfully back to the boat. Russell was at the ladder, half pushing, half coaxing the strong-shouldered red-haired teenager up ahead of him into Will's waiting arms.

Raif trod water, waiting, too numb now to feel the cold. The lovely face, with its strong cheekbones and straight nose, that was cradled on his shoulder could have been made of marble or wax, it seemed so cold, lifeless and still, and the eyes and mouth were closed as if the sculptor of the marble hadn't imagined jewel-coloured irises or pearly teeth beneath those lids and lips.

But she was alive. Raif could feel the heartbeat pulsing under her breast where his arm supported her. Then he felt a tangle of something soft and floating around his left arm. What was it? Blonde hair, a long thick mass of it.

'Ready?' It was Russell, calling down from the deck. He was reaching a hand down to pull her up.

'She's unconscious,' Raif said, and then somehow, half a minute later, they were up the ladder and on the deck. He was kneeling, and she was in his arms, as the engine throbbed beneath them, powering them away from the stricken ship and back to shore.

A green dress, the blue-green of a stormy sea hit by a sudden shaft of sunlight, was wound around the lower half of her body. It had slipped from her shoulders, twisted and sopping, and only the long curling tendrils of blonde hair kept the cold rounded shapes of her breasts from being uncovered. The dress imprisoned her legs tightly.

As he stared down at her, knowing that he had only a few seconds more in which to recover his breath before he must start to assess and treat her condition, she stirred. He heard a sound of surprise and strangely eager relief escaped from deep in his own chest, and saw a brief glimpse of eyes that were grey in this light. A mermaid, she was. That dress making a tail, that hair, and something magic about her. . .

Then she lapsed into a deeper unconsciousness again, and was still. Will Thomas appeared as Raif braced himself and stood up with her still in his arms.

'Raif. . .?' Will croaked.

'She looks like a mermaid, Will, don't you think?' Raif said, chafing and cradling her to start to bring warmth into her again.

Then he saw, with a pang of intuitive dread and foreboding, how very ill the old doctor looked. . .

Karen Madigan blinked and screwed up her eyes as she emerged from the hospital and into the warm sun and breeze of a day in late May. Discharged. Convalescent. Free! She ran a pale, thin hand through the patchy mass of blonde hair that she still wasn't used to. Part of it was shaved, at the back over near her left ear where she'd received the blow, during the failed lifeboat launch, that had kept her in a coma for almost two weeks. Part of it had simply been snipped off at about shoulder length for convenience during nursing care.

Being a doctor herself, she had known exactly why it had to be done, but it was still a shock. She'd had her long luxurious tresses for so many years, and to have the decision to lose them taken out of her hands like that. . .

'I'll at least get a proper cut,' she said to herself as she stood uncertainly on the hospital steps. A good hairdresser should be able to style it to disguise that stubbly shaved bit, with its pinkly healing scar, until the hair grew back as good as ever.

Was there a good hairdresser on Long Beach Peninsula? It seemed ridiculous that it was this she was wondering about. Here she was, about as directionless as a human being could be. Even her clothes consisted of basic jeans, a long-sleeved cotton jersey and functional leather sandals, purchased on her behalf by a hospital volunteer. Surely there ought to be other things uppermost in her mind? Her whole future, for example.

None the less, half an hour later she was ensconced in a black vinyl chair belonging to Suzanne's Coiffure, facing her reflection in a large mirror.

'Just visiting?' asked the spiky-haired brunette in her mid-twenties—doubtless Suzanne herself—as she coaxed Karen's head back towards the basin and began running strong needles of warm water through the blonde strands.

'I. . . I don't really know what I'm doing,' Karen said with sudden doubt. 'I was on the *Star of Scandinavia*.'

'Oh. . .'

The whole of Long Beach Peninsula had been aware of the disaster, but Karen had had the uneasy sensation, since coming to full consciousness several days ago, that the event was already in the past. Three people had died—an elderly widower, and two of the ship's Norwegian crew, who had been down in the engine-room when the explosion that holed the ship had occurred.

Doubtless in some part of the world grief for these men was still very fresh and real, but it had not touched the residents of the Long Beach area. Karen had been the last of the injured to leave the hospital, and none of her possessions had been salvaged.

The tide had started to rise after the last boatload of passengers was safely clear of the vessel, and it had freed itself from the sand bar on which it had temporarily grounded, and drifted heavily through the huge swell before sinking for good in deeper water. A major salvage operation would be needed if it was ever to be brought to the surface.

It seemed months rather than weeks since Karen had stood on the deck watching the Oregon coast slipping by, and waiting for the onset of the storm they could see approaching from the north-west. She had been with Stefan Torsten on the deck that evening. He was the ship's second officer, new to the *Star of Scandinavia* that season, and it had been looking as if a romance might be starting to develop between them. . .

But Stefan was gone now, back to Norway, having left no message, and he already seemed so unreal to Karen that it didn't matter. In the two years since her mother's death at home in England, she had grown used to a sense of being alone in the world. And she had taken the job as medical officer on the *Star of Scandinavia* partly to quell a restlessness that had been threatening to surface even before the long sadness of her mother's illness, so she was not as unprepared for her present situation as many young women of twenty-eight might have been.

There were certain undeniably pressing questions, however. Absently, she watched as the hairdresser studied her head of blonde hair.

'Yes, I can cover it easily enough,' the girl said. 'But I can't give you any choice, I'm afraid. It's going to look layered and fluffy and a little asymmetrical, and that's that.'

'It sounds fine,' Karen said, nodding, then her thoughts wandered again as Suzanne began her work with the scissors.

I've lost weight, she realised. And I'm paler than ever. A cruise ship doctor didn't have as much chance to soak up the sun as many people imagined, and it was only the very beginning of summer. If I were my doctor, I'd say I need a couple of weeks of thorough rest.

She had, in fact, been told this at the hospital, but it hadn't really sunk in until now. Her recovery after emerging from the coma had been rapid, and she bore no long-term effects from her injury, but it was important not to overestimate her strength.

Gradually a plan began to sketch itself in her mind. She would have her rest right here on the Long Beach Peninsula. First she'd go to Seattle—tomorrow perhaps—and settle her affairs—replacement passport and papers, insurance and salary pay-out from the shipping company, Scan-line. . . Then she'd buy some clothes, rent a car, come back here and make a serious attempt to convalesce.

'There!' The hairdresser stood back and surveyed her work.

Karen returned her still-fuzzy mind to the present, and took in a surprised breath. It looked fabulous, and very different—a sophisticated, yet surprisingly casual bob, light and easy to care for. The girl held up the mirror behind, so that Karen could see the back.

'It'll need a careful brush at first, to keep it in place, and some styling mousse, but really you'd never know that scar was there.'

'No, you wouldn't. That's marvellous!' Karen stood

up happily, then clutched the chair for support as she was seized with sudden dizziness.

For a fraction of a second, an image. . .no, more than that, a sense-memory, flashed through her mind. Wetness, cold, arms holding her, a man's face, and a word spoken that she couldn't grasp, but somehow it was connected with fairytales. It wasn't the first time this had happened. It had seized her twice in the hospital as well. It was disturbing. Then it faded.

'Are you all right?' Suzanne asked.

'I just got out of hospital an hour ago,' Karen confessed.

'Oh, my stars!' the girl exclaimed. 'And what are you going to do now?'

'I'm not quite sure,' Karen confessed again. 'I'd like to find a motel. . .'

The Clambake Motel was very much a small family concern—Suzanne's family, to be precise—her aunt and uncle, June and Les Price. Karen surveyed the cosy room she had been shown to. It was almost a cabin, in fact—the last room in the block, containing kitchenette as well as bathroom, and two lounge chairs as well as bed and television. With tea-making things and a frozen TV dinner provided by June Price, it seemed to Karen that night that she had all she could reasonably ask for.

A week later, that feeling hadn't changed. It had been a fairly solitary week, apart from casual exchanges with the Prices and with Suzanne, who dropped in one evening to see how she was getting on. The bus trip to Seattle had been exhausting, underlining again her real need for a rest, but things had gone smoothly, and the pay-out from the Norwegian shipping line had been larger than she had expected. Added to her careful savings over the past few years, and to a small inheritance from her mother, it meant a nice nest-egg. But what for? Just to sit in the bank?

A night in one of Seattle's most comfortable hotels had restored her energy, and the journey back to Long Beach had been smooth and untroubled in the small yellow car she had hired.

The rest of the week? Walks on the beach, exploratory trips in the car, lazy sessions in the grassy stretch of garden beyond the motel veranda with a book. . . There was a delightful peace and freshness about this place that seemed to be slowly working its way into her soul.

The peninsula was fairly flat, nothing more than an enormous tongue of sand, but with the ocean on one side and a bay on the other, scrub-covered sandhills and modest seaward-facing houses, many of them belonging to summer visitors, it had the full flavour and drama of the sea.

It was on Monday morning that she saw the notice. She had been shopping in the small township of Ocean Park, and was walking back to the car with her bag of provisions when her eyes strayed to the window of a modest wooden building: 'Medical Practice For Immediate Sale'.

When a woman in her late thirties answered Karen's knock at the door, she felt like running away as if she'd been a child caught in fulfilling a dare, but her voice was quite steady when she spoke.

'I saw your notice in the window, and I'd like to find out a little more about it.'

'Come in.' The woman's voice was toneless and tired.

'Is the practice still for sale?'

'Yes, it is.' They entered what was clearly the surgery. 'Do sit down. My name's Gloria Denny.'

She removed some untidy papers from a chair, put them on a cluttered desk and ran a distracted hand through hair that had been dyed an unsuccessful dark burgundy to disguise early greying.

Karen glanced uncertainly towards the window. The day was bright outside, but the blinds were down and an electric light glowed from the ceiling. Mrs Denny caught the look and rose again hastily from her chair behind the desk.

'I'm sorry. . . I got here early this morning,' she said, and Karen felt guilty that her face had been so easy to read.

Still, it was a relief to see the room by natural light. The initial impression of dinginess that Karen had had was inaccurate. It was actually a pleasant and well-looked-after room. She guessed that it was Gloria Denny who had created the untidiness today while going through things.

'So you're interested in the practice?' Mrs Denny asked.

'Yes,' Karen answered abruptly. Was she? If not, then she was here under false pretences. Perhaps that knock at the door had been nothing but an absurd impulse.

'Well, I'm certainly keen to sell it as soon as possible,' the older woman blurted. She was clearly under some sort of strain, her rather dumpy body held rigidly and her fingers picking nervously at the collar of her cream blouse. Karen found her twitchiness contagious and had to fold her hands in her lap to stop herself from fiddling with the hem of her own slim forest-green skirt.

But Mrs Denny was speaking again now. 'You see, my husband has had some business problems. . .'

'Business problems? What kind of a doctor is he?' Karen asked quickly. It sounded more than a little suspicious.

'Oh, my husband's not a doctor!' Gloria exclaimed. 'I

should have made it clear. This was my father's practice . . .Dr William Thomas. . .but he died unexpectedly——' she choked for a moment over the word '—over three weeks ago. My husband runs a business. . .'

She went on for some time about seasonal slumps, realisable assets, the value of the property, surgical equipment, patient records, the formalities of the will and her father's lawyer, and finally named a price that to Karen's ears sounded very reasonable.

'Are you interested?' She leaned across the desk, her face creased in a careworn frown, then sat back abruptly, as if recollecting an earlier lesson in selling techniques, and added quickly, 'Of course, I've had several other enquiries.'

'Of course.' Karen nodded, while thinking privately, She hasn't at all. And I'll bet she only put up the notice this morning. Poor Mr Denny's business *must* be bad.

Just bad, or crooked as well? That wasn't her affair, but she would certainly examine this place thoroughly, make a few careful enquiries, and talk to Dr Thomas's lawyer before she made any sort of commitment. . .

Karen brought herself up short. How ridiculous! This had been a casual enquiry, an absurd impulse, and now she was acting as if she really was seriously considering the option. Well, she could certainly afford it. That nestegg, some of it sitting in a new bank account in Seattle and the rest still in England. . .

And it would help that, in spite of a thoroughly English unbringing, she was actually an American citizen, through the Chicago-born father she hadn't seen for twenty-five years, after her parents' bitter divorce.

No! Stop this! It was an insane idea!

And yet she had to do something with her future. Did it make any more sense to go back to England? Or to wait until Scan-line found a job for her on one of its other cruise ships? They'd made it clear that that could be months away, and, in any case, she'd never seen herself as remaining a shipboard medical officer for life.

She realised that Gloria Denny was studying her, with a searching and anxious expression in her pale blue eyes. 'It's not a decision I can make on the spur of the moment, naturally,' Karen said.

'Naturally,' Mrs Denny echoed, her tone dropping in disappointment.

Karen felt a sudden spurt of mingled irritation and compassion. Good heavens! It seemed as if the woman had hoped to see the money deposited in cash on top of the messy desk right here and now! Things must be bad for Denny and Company! There was real grief somewhere there, too, for Dr Thomas. This must be hard for Gloria Denny.

Karen stood up, and immediately Mrs Denny had risen and come round the side of the desk to shake hands. She was short, only a little over five feet, and against Karen's willowy five feet ten the impression that she was a pleading supplicant, with Karen in the role of potential favour-giver, was only enhanced.

'May I see your lawyer tomorrow?' Karen heard herself ask.

'My father's lawyer, it will be,' Mrs Denny said eagerly. 'Yes, yes, I'm sure you can. Shall we say first thing? Nine?'

'Hadn't you better——?' Karen began.

'Oh, I'll check it with him and contact you by phone if it's not suitable. Here.' She took a card from the pocket of her blouse and thrust it into Karen's hand. 'This is his address.'

'Thank you.' Karen smiled, aware that she was at her most English and her most polite.

Mrs Denny seemed to have no curiosity, however, about what an English doctor might doing in Long

Beach, casually enquiring about a medical practice. Really, it was ridiculous to assume that you could sell a practice through a notice in the window, as if you were selling a second-hand car in a surburban driveway.

Ridiculous, and yet it looked as if Gloria Denny might have found her buyer.

'I'm staying at the Clambake Motel, if you do need to change the appointment. I'm sure the number will be in the telephone directory,' Karen told her.

She was ushered to the door and shown deferentially down the street, with several goodbyes and anxious reminders about the nine o'clock appointment. If Karen hadn't suggested the meeting with Dr Thomas's lawyer, the whole thing might have been dismissed an hour later as an idle whim, but she was committed to giving it serious thought now.

With a wry expression, Dr Karen Madigan addressed herself aloud as she prepared a salad roll for lunch in her motel unit.

'You'd better get some bracing air this afternoon, my girl. I think you're still under the influence of that blow on the head!'

CHAPTER TWO

THE day's early brightness hadn't fulfilled its promise, Dr Raiford Calvert found when he emerged from his surgery at three and locked the door. He gave himself an early finish on Mondays—and Thursdays too—because he had scheduled consulting hours again between seven and nine in the evening on those days. Mostly he was finished by two or two-thirty, but today he was a little later than usual.

In his four-week absence, people seemed to have been hoarding up their ailments, waiting for his return, in spite of the fact that he'd organised a locum from Portland to fill in for him, and his receptionist had been inundated with requests for appointments this morning. It was flattering, but still, he wasn't the only doctor on Long Beach Peninsula.

Raif's breath caught in his throat for a moment as this thought came to him. There was one doctor less now. Will's death, in spite of that moment of foreboding on the coastguard boat, had come as a shock twenty-four hours later. There was no doubt that the strain and exhaustion of the hours of rescue work had taken their toll and hastened the onset of that fatal heart attack.

Raif had been the man Will had called, gasping in pain down the phone, then letting the instrument drop. By the time Raif had covered the few miles at a screeching pace in his old car, it was already too late. Thank God he'd been able to attend the funeral, at least. Will's daughter Gloria had made all the arrangements for it by phone, but a piece of ghastly bad luck—an aircraft delay and a missed connection—had stopped her from getting from Texas to Long Beach in time.

The next day, Raif himself had been on a plane, bound for Los Angeles for a four-week—well, vacation wasn't quite the word. He hadn't enjoyed the trip, and that wasn't only because he'd been mourning for Will. Arriving back in Long Beach last night, he was convinced that the time in Los Angeles hadn't solved or clarified anything.

What he needed now, he thought, surveying the grey sky sceptically, was a long walk on the beach. He drove north, almost to Ocean Park, then turned west on a side road and parked his car in a sandy clearing amid scrubby trees that sheltered behind long, vegetation-covered sandhills.

The wind hit him stingingly in the face when he breasted the high ridge of sand and saw the rolling breakers of the Pacific thudding on to the shore. The beach was deserted, thank the lord. Often Raif felt he'd gladly exchange a sunny sky for bad weather and the solitude it brought him on these sands. He shrugged into a grey windproof jacket, turned the collar up, thrust his hands into the hip-level pockets and strode barefoot with dark trousers rolled to the calves along the hard sand at the water's edge.

He had been walking steadily for half an hour, lost in thoughts that were at times circular and frustrating, at times optimistic and satisfying, when he saw a figure coming towards him from the opposite direction, just a dot of red walking at a pace less brisk than his own.

It was a woman, he realised about five minutes later, still some distance off. He watched the horizon for a while. He couldn't go on staring at her until they met! Then when he focused his gaze on her again, he was surprised to find that they were now only about ten yards apart. She must have quickened her pace.

'Look! I'm so thrilled!' she called out to him suddenly, flourishing a spherical object, and then she had halted in front of him, her green-grey eyes shining and her lightly tanned cheeks flushed with excitement. 'A Japanese glass fishing float!' she added unnecessarily.

'Yes, it's a very nice one too,' Raif said, nodding.

It was about ten inches in diameter, the colour of the sea itself, a thick rich-looking glass with irregular ripples and flows that only added to the impression it gave of having been made in some magic under-sea glassworks. She held it out to him and he took it, gazing into it and running his hands over its surface as if it were a fortune-teller's crystal ball.

'I'm so excited!' she repeated. 'I thought they were quite rare.'

'They are, these days.' He looked up at her as he handed it back, and watched her hold it carefully in both hands, her slim fingers splayed evenly. The rust-red wool jacket she wore contrasted with her spiky, fluffy blonde hair, and, like him, she wore dark trousers that were rolled to the calf so that she could feel the sand and an advancing edge of sea foam on her cold bare feet.

'You've been lucky,' he added.

'I know,' she agreed. 'The people at the motel where I'm staying have several of them. They told me almost all the Japanese trawlers use plastic floats these days, and the ones washed up on shore here could have been riding the Pacific Ocean currents for years and years.'

'That's true,' Raif answered. 'There was a strong westerly last night. Still blowing actually, though it's dying now. That's what usually brings them in.'

So she was a tourist! he was thinking as he spoke. English too, clearly. Funny for a woman her age to be wandering this deserted beach alone so early in the season. People usually came here with family. Perhaps she didn't have one. There was no ring on her finger.

'Well, I dare say you think I'm a bit mad—crazy—gabbling at a total stranger in the middle of a beach, but I had to share my triumph,' she said with bright eyes and a frank smile.

'You're not crazy,' he answered. 'I quite understand.'

'Thank you! Goodbye, then,' she called, already on her way.

'Goodbye. . .' He turned back to her and they waved, then each moved on in opposite directions, alone.

Raif's eyes settled on the flat line of the horizon again. Two different greys today, sky and sea, yet still endlessly changing and full of interest. He tried to remember what he had been thinking about before that rust-red jacket had impinged on his world, but he couldn't. For no reason, he thought back to the night, now four weeks distant, when the *Star of Scandinavia* had gone down.

It wasn't the first time he'd caught his breath at that one memory—the memory of the woman in green with the hair and limbs and sea-born mystery of a mermaid. . .Why should he think of that now?

Karen Madigan kept smiling for several minutes as she walked. She was tempted to turn back and look at him again, but she didn't. Was he a local? He hadn't said anything to make her think so. The Prices had already made it clear to her that there were a number of important classifications at work among the population of Long Beach. There were old-timers, locals, residents, visitors, summer people and tourists. . .

The stranger, who had been so gratifyingly full of understanding about her excitement over the glass float, didn't fall obviously into any of those categories at first glance, though he must belong to one of them. He was attractive, she decided dispassionately, with his broad shoulders, dark windblown hair, high, strongly moulded cheekbones, and firm sensitive mouth. He looked intelligent too. That impression came clearly though his grey eyes. Perhaps he was a celebrity on retreat in this distant region, she wondered suddenly, because his face had looked vaguely familiar, as if she had seen it before somewhere. In a magazine?

There was a chance, of course, that she would find out the answer to these questions, if the man did live in this area, because he might one day come to her as a patient...Hang on a minute! Did this mean she had made her decision?

With her heart giving several surprising thuds, Karen realised that it did. She had been walking for an hour and a half now, and was nearly back to the place where she had parked her car. This was fortunate, because she was growing very tired. She had spent most of that hour and a half up and back along the beach, thinking about the question of Gloria Denny's medical practice, and, whichever way she looked at it, she had liked the idea.

If tomorrow's meeting with the late Dr Thomas's lawyer went off successfully, and if the enquiries she intended to make on her own produced satisfactory results, the brass plate beside the door of that modern wooden building would read 'Dr Karen Madigan' very soon.

When Karen reached the small yellow rental car, she placed the hollow sea-green glass ball carefully on the floor in the front seat and wrapped her jacket around it, as if swaddling a baby in a woollen rug. She knew that the stranger on the beach, even though he had been warm and friendly, could not really have fully understood what the piece of sea-debris meant to her.

It was a symbol and an omen—a sign that she would put down roots in this salt-tanged corner of the world. Other than the basic wardrobe of half a dozen mix-and-match garments she had bought in Seattle, it was the first possession she had acquired since the ship went down, and it seemed fitting somehow that, like herself, it had been washed haphazardly on to the shores of this place. Yes, she and the glass ball had both arrived at Long Beach through unconventional channels.

'I'm going to look after you,' Karen said to the ball as she started the car. 'Pity you can't do the same for me, isn't it?'

'Dr Madigan...' It was a man of about fifty who rose from behind his desk to greet her the next morning after Gloria Denny, dressed dumpily in a dark suit, had led the way nervously into his office.

He was very tall, rather ungainly, and it seemed to take him some little time to fully uncurl into a standing position. He studied her as he did so, but the bristling grey-tinged brows lowered over his brown eyes didn't fully disguise the sceptical assessment in his gaze. Karen was surprised when she read the look. Surely she was the one who should be sceptical? This was hardly the most usual way for a medical practice to change hands.

'I'm Henry Sewell, as of course you've gathered,' he went on, reaching out a large hand, which Karen dutifully shook as she murmured a conventional greeting. 'Lawyer acting for the late William Thomas, and now for his daughter Gloria.'

He inclined his head towards Mrs Denny, who had seated herself already, and was fiddling with the clasp on her brown leather clutch-bag. Karen smoothed her forest-green skirt and sat down too, in the one remaining chair.

'Now, I understand that you wish to buy the practice, Dr Madigan.'

'No...' Karen glanced sharply at Gloria Denny, who opened her mouth and then shut it again tremulously. 'That's putting it in much too concrete a way. I've expressed some interest. I'll need to find out many more facts before I make a final decision.'

'Ah, I understood you had made some enquiries earlier,' Mr Sewell murmured.

'Earlier?' Karen felt annoyed. What did he mean by that? Yesterday morning was 'earlier' and her short interview with Mrs Denny decidedly constituted an 'enquiry', but it was scarcely enough on which to base this sort of major life decision. It sounded as if Gloria had given an exaggerated description of her interest. 'That's true,' she said, after a short pause. There was no sense in creating an issue out of the thing. 'But I'd like to see all the relevant papers, title deeds, Health Department records, and so forth.'

'Of course,' Mr Sewell agreed, still studying her. 'Although you'll find that everything is quite in order. Dr Thomas was a thoroughly professional man.'

'And I am a thoroughly professional woman.' Karen smiled.

'As you should be,' Mr Sewell conceded. 'Mrs Denny is anxious to get this business settled as quickly as possible, but of course there are legal complexities. She points out that it will be difficult for Dr Thomas's patients if the surgery is closed for an extended period, and I think we'll be able to come to an interim arrangement whereby you would function—how can I put it?—well, as a locum in the practice until it was legally your own. That is if, as you have said, you do in fact decide to purchase.'

Karen nodded. A locum arrangement made sense. Contracts and conveyancing took time. Property didn't change hands in a day. But Henry Sewell was speaking deliberately again, this time to Mrs Denny.

'Gloria, I think you can go now. I expect you have other things to attend to. . .'

'Yes.' She leaned forward. 'But I'd like to know as soon as——'

'Of course,' Mr Sewell interrupted smoothly, rising to

his feet ready to usher her out. She seemed a little reluctant to leave, as if she didn't trust Mr Sewell to be sufficiently encouraging to Karen. When the door had shut behind her, Mr Sewell returned to his desk and sat down again with a sigh. He leaned his elbows on the desk's wooden surface, pressed his fingertips together neatly and took in a deep breath.

'Mrs Denny is creating a bad impression, I think,' he said carefully. 'I'm not really in a position to comment, as I'm sure you'll appreciate, but I gather her husband's business is in trouble, and he's keen for her to realise a capital sum from her father's estate as soon as possible. I can assure you that there is absolutely nothing wrong with either the land, the building or the medical side of the thing. I'm not entirely happy, frankly, with the way she's choosing to proceed, but you need not concern yourself with these family matters. If you wish to buy the practice when I've answered all your questions, I'm happy for us to go ahead.'

His comments, couched in a lawyer's habitually cautious and complex turn of phrase, sounded quite reasonable. At ten o'clock the following morning, Karen told him by telephone that she was ready to make a commitment.

The rest of the week wasn't quite the lazy, convalescence she had envisaged two weeks earlier. She had decided to open the surgery on Monday afternoon, which left her with scarcely a spare minute in the intervening five days. She had to find somewhere to live, buy a car, arrrange for the transfer of her money from England. . . The list went on.

When she unlocked the front door of the surgery at eleven on Monday morning, Karen wondered whether she had been wise to start work so soon. It was rather unsettling to be alone here, and wandering around the five-roomed building with little to do but acclimatise until Dr Thomas's receptionist, Barbara Stenlow, arrived at one.

Gloria Denny had been busy here on Friday, Karen realised, after she had opened the blinds to let bright sunlight flood into the place, bringing out the deep burnt orange colour of the spring-weight wool dress she wore. The surgery itself was tidy now, no longer cluttered with the personal papers belonging to Dr Thomas that Gloria had been sorting on Karen's first visit—only a week ago!

The waiting-room looked fresh and clean too. The magazines were piled neatly with the newest ones on top, the grey carpet had been vacuumed, the dark blue fabric of the chairs brushed, and surfaces and sills wiped. There were even fresh flowers on the receptionist's desk. And a card. Karen read it. 'Wishing you every success, Gloria Denny.'

It was a nice touch, and Karen smiled. Her initial slightly negative impression of the dumpy woman had been revised during their successive meetings last week. It seemed that Bruce Denny was the real problem, and that his 'business troubles' were the result of reckless dabbling on the verge of illegal activity. Now Gloria was having to step in to pick up the pieces.

Karen came across the answer-machine connected to the phone, pressed a button and heard Gloria's voice.

'You have reached Dr Thomas's surgery. Dr Karen Madigan will be taking over the practice, but until Monday the surgery will be unattended. For alternative assistance, please contact Shoalwater Hospital or Dr Raiford Calvert at Klipsan Beach. If you have a message for Dr Madigan, please leave it after the tone.'

Karen pressed another button and heard two clicks and several pips, but there were no messages. She was a little surprised. She had thought that a couple of people might have left telephone numbers and requests for an appointment. Still, many people were nervous about answering machines.

She sat down at the desk to compose her own message for when the surgery was unattended in the future, but stopped, feeling foolish and frustrated when she had written the words 'For urgent assistance after hours please call. . .' She didn't know her own telephone number! For that matter, she couldn't at the moment remember her street address. Was it 21 or 25 Oyster Road?

The estate agent had shown her over several places on Saturday morning and she had settled on a tiny cottage perched on heavy stilt-like footings so that it overlooked a sandhill, an expanse of grey sandy beach and the endless swell of the Pacific beyond. She had rejected an ultra-modern apartment in the heart of Klipsan Beach, and a much larger free-standing house crowded among others near the main road in Nahcotta. Perhaps it was a foolish choice, but she had no possessions with which to fill a larger place, and there had been an atmosphere about the more isolated beach-front cottage that had appealed, in spite of its spartan nature. She had got the key to it this morning and checked out of her now-familiar room at the Clambake Motel, with promises to the Prices to keep them in touch with how she was settling in. She would unpack her meagre collection of belongings at the cottage this evening after work at the surgery had finished.

And tonight she would definitely take note of both the street number and the telephone number at her new home. The new answer-machine message would have to wait until tomorrow. She took a tiny notepad from her bag and added this to a list of 'Things To Do'.

I *have* launched into things too soon, Karen thought. The list looked daunting in length and she felt tired just looking at it. At least she had had the sense to schedule surgery hours only in the afternoons this week.

Karen continued her tour of the small building. The patients' changing-room and bathroom were spick and span, as was the fourth room on the premises, which served as a store for equipment and medication as well as a wash-room and sterilisation area for Karen and her assistant.

The fifth room, a sizeable space which Dr Thomas didn't seem to have used for anything much, was now swept bare and clean, and Karen decided she would like to do something more imaginative with it than simply fill it with old piles of medical journals and other junk. Not that she had any junk at the moment anyway.

Arriving back at the waiting-room, Karen decided there was little more to do until Barbara Stenlow arrived at one, and she was on the point of going out to pick up a light lunch from a take-away place down the road, when the phone rang.

'Dr Madigan's surgery,' Karen said crisply.

'Oh, I thought I was calling Dr Thomas,' a woman's voice said on the other end of the line.

'I'm afraid Dr Thomas died a few weeks ago, and I've taken over his practice.'

'Oh! Oh, dear, I'm terribly sorry. I just looked it up in the phone book. I'm only here for a week, but I seem to have come up in an awful rash. . .'

The woman asked if Dr Madigan could 'fit her in' at half-past three, and Karen resisted the temptation to confess that, actually, she could fit her in at any time between one and five. She lingered in the surgery for a few minutes after the call, half hoping that it was like spring's first cuckoo, a harbinger of things to come, but the phone stayed silent and she knew she was being foolish. The appointment had buoyed her spirits, however, and the walk to the take-away bar in her bright new dress was thoroughly enjoyable.

Barbara Stenlow was in the surgery when Karen returned. It was quite a shock. She appeared in the surgery doorway with a feathery potted fern in her hands just as Karen closed the outer door behind her, and the new doctor nearly jumped out of her skin.

'Did I startle you?' the older woman said. 'I have my own key, of course, and I came early to make sure everything was in order.'

'So did I,' Karen confessed. 'Then I popped out for some lunch.'

It was an awkward first meeting, when they had only spoken briefly on the phone, and Karen had the uneasy feeling that Miss Stenlow was holding something back, wasn't being as friendly as one might have hoped and expected. Of course she was upset about Dr Thomas's death, but did that mean she couldn't extend a welcome to the doctor who had stepped in to take his place?

'Have we no appointments?' Barbara Stenlow was asking. She opened a drawer in the desk and took out a large red vinyl-covered book, opening it with an expert flick at today's page.

'Of course, yes, we do, how stupid of me!' Karen exclaimed as she looked at the appointment book. 'I should have written it in.'

'Just one, then?' Miss Stenlow asked abruptly, snapping the book shut again.

'Yes, at half-past three,' Karen answered slowly. Was it her imagination, or did the woman sound pleased that the afternoon was so empty? 'I'm sorry, I should have written it in,' she repeated nervously. 'But I wasn't thinking.'

Inwardly, her heart was sinking. Don't tell me we're not going to get on! she thought heavily. Their dresses clashed dreadfully, for a start. Barbara Stenlow was wearing Wedgwood-blue, which went rather well with her dark, grey-threaded hair and slate-blue eyes—and with the carpets and furnishings too—but looked horrible against Karen's deep burnt orange.

'Half-past three,' Barbara echoed.

'She's a tourist with a rash,' Karen added, helpfully and unnecessarily. Again, Barbara echoed the key words.

'A tourist. . .'

She looked quietly pleased now, and Karen felt sick with disappointment. What was going on? There was a definite veiled coolness in Miss Stenlow's manner, and Karen had been counting so much on having support from her receptionist. It was an important role in a small practice like this one, and didn't Miss Stenlow have the imagination to see that Karen had some difficult settling-in to do? It couldn't do Dr Thomas any good to be frosty and unhelpful towards his successor.

Karen stood uncertainly in the middle of the waiting-room. Miss Stenlow placed the potted fern carefully on one of the low tables, moving a pile of magazines to one side, then turned to her new employer.

'Why don't you wait in the surgery?' she said. 'I can take any calls that come in now.'

'But if I have any questions. . .?' Karen asked a little desperately. She had imagined sitting down and having a cup of coffee and a cosy chat with Barbara, in which she found out all sorts of small details about the practice and about Long Beach that couldn't possibly be discovered through direct, formal questioning.

'The intercom is on your desk,' Barbara Stenlow said, and Karen almost laughed. She could just hear herself pressing the buzzer and then asking in a chatty tone through the speaker, 'How long have you lived in Long Beach, Barbara?'

'All right,' she managed finally. 'And we discussed surgery hours for the rest of the week over the phone, didn't we? The same as today—one till five. If anyone rings for an appointment. . .'

'Yes.' Barbara nodded dismissively, as if it was naïve to think that there would be any appointments at all.

Karen took refuge in the surgery. It was distinctly boring. After ten minutes, she opened the drawers of the desk and found the latest issue of a medical journal, which she opened in relief. Soon she was absorbed. On a cruise ship, it was hard to keep thoroughly up to date with new research and methods.

It was some time later when there was a tap at the door and Barbara's head appeared around the end of it. Not the half-past three appointment already? No.

'Would you like a hot drink?' Barbara enquired.

'Mmm, lovely,' Karen answered.

'I expect you'd prefer tea. English people usually do.'

'Yes, please,' Karen said, nodding. She didn't care whether it was tea or coffee, she simply felt an uncomfortable eagerness to get on Barbara's right side somehow. And she certainly wasn't going to bother to explain that she *wasn't* English, when she felt very thoroughly at the moment that she *was*!

'I don't think we've got any,' Barbara said, and Karen flushed. Was she being over-sensitive in suspecting that Miss Stenlow had worded her question deliberately so that Karen ended up asking for something that was unavailable? She controlled herself carefully.

'Coffee will be fine, then.' But she couldn't resist an addition. 'With milk. . .if you've got it.'

She returned to an article about Sudden Infant Death Syndrome, and gave only a brief thanks when the coffee was placed quietly at her elbow. The phone rang twice outside in the waiting-room while she was drinking it, but the intercom didn't buzz. Two appointments? Karen hoped so very much, but she wasn't going to betray her eagerness by asking.

The half-past three appointment came and went. It was clearly just a mild allergy, a rash accompanied by puffy eyes and intermittent sneezing, and Karen prescribed a new anti-histamine, said to be free from the side-effect of drowsiness that had reduced the usefulness of the drug in the past.

At a quarter past four she couldn't bear sitting in the surgery alone any longer, and went out to the waiting-room.

'Any appointments for later in the week?' she asked casually.

'One on Wednesday at two,' Barbara said. She didn't mention the three other phone calls that had come in during the afternoon.

'You might as well go, then, Miss Stenlow,' Karen said, in as friendly a tone as she could. She waited for the other woman to say, 'Oh, please call me Barbara,' but Miss Stenlow didn't, although they would be less than a generation apart in age, and America was not a notably formal country.

Instead, Miss Stenlow merely nodded briefly and gathered her bag and light jacket. 'Will you be here to open up tomorrow, or shall I?' she asked.

'Oh, I will,' Karen said quickly. 'That's fine.'

'Well, I'll see you then. Goodbye.' Barbara's controlled mouth widened in the briefest of false smiles, and then she was gone.

Karen stood at the desk, leaning her hands on it and feeling her head drumming. She couldn't go on behaving in that eager, deferential way, as if she were an office junior trying to live down some early mistake. It was sickening to think of it, but if she didn't find a way to make their relationship improve, and if Barbara didn't meet her halfway, then Karen would have to find someone new.

There was a sharp rap at the door and she turned in

relief to answer it, somehow expecting it to be Barbara herself, armed with an apology. But it wasn't Barbara. . .
It was the man she had seen on the beach last Monday.

CHAPTER THREE

BEFORE she could stop herself, Karen smiled widely. 'Oh, hello!'

Her voice was warm and welcoming. She had thought of the stranger several times since that chance meeting on the sand, and thought of him as an ally, in spite of the brevity of their contact.

'Oh, it's you,' he answered gruffly, seeming embarrassed somehow, while acknowledging that he too remembered their other encounter. Karen assumed that his gruff tone was the result of the surprise that she had felt as well. 'Can I come in?'

'Well—er——' She hesitated. It was one thing to meet a man in the middle of a beach and have a casual, friendly word or two. It was quite another to closet herself in a room with him. His good looks hadn't broken down her reserve to *that* extent.

'I'm Dr Calvert,' he said. 'Raiford Calvert.'

'Oh, of course, the name Miss Stenlow left on the machine,' Karen said, her brow clearing and a smile lighting up her face again as she stood aside for him to pass into the small entrance passage that led to the waiting-room.

As she closed the door behind her and followed him she felt a wonderful relief. Today hadn't been easy, and she still had to settle into her new home later on tonight. But if she had found a friend in her own profession, a supportive colleague, that would make a big difference.

'I'm so glad it's you!' she blurted too eagerly, when they faced each other in the waiting-room. 'This past week has been rather hectic, and today was a little discouraging. It's lovely of you to drop in. . .'

She stopped. He was looking at her strangely, as if he wanted to stop her from talking but didn't know quite how to do it. He was dressed casually in pale grey trousers, darker grey shirt and a light wool pullover, also in tones of grey, and he had his hands on his hips. His strong jaw was thrust forward a little and a heavy frown made a crease above his cool grey eyes. Suddenly, it didn't look in the least as if he'd just dropped in to welcome a new colleague.

'I only heard this morning what you'd done,' he said abruptly, and took a few restless paces in the room.

'What I'd done?' Karen echoed stupidly. 'You mean buying the practice?'

'You haven't bought it yet,' he answered quickly. 'There's still plenty of time to pull out.'

'But I don't want to pull out.' Karen thudded heavily into one of the low dark blue waiting-room chairs. She was completely bewildered by this sudden attack, and, on top of Barbara's unfriendliness and all the events of the past month or more, she was starting to feel somewhat persecuted.

'Of course you don't, but I'm asking you to, all the same.' He pulled a second chair towards him, raking its moulded metal legs across the carpet, and sat down, leaning forward.

'Why?' Karen asked, her voice rising beyond her control. Perhaps it *was* what she wanted to do—give up the practice and leave Long Beach, get away from the mess that had loomed up this afternoon, out of the blue and totally out of her understanding.

'That practice was meant for me, and I think you know that,' Raiford was saying.

'How was it meant for you?' Karen asked.

'Wasn't it you who rang Will Thomas almost six weeks ago asking if the practice was for sale?'

'No, it wasn't,' Karen said.

'Then it must have been. . . But that doesn't make sense. . .' His words trailed off.

Karen spoke again, more forcefully. 'Six weeks ago, in fact, I'd barely heard of Long Beach.'

There was a silence, and she looked up at him after lowering her gaze to study her fingernails. He was examining her intently.

'Perhaps I've been too hasty, then,' he said slowly.

'Please explain this whole thing from the beginning, Dr Calvert.'

'Yes, I think I'd better.'

Karen sat back a little, and some of her tension eased. Surely things could be straightened out, and they would end up friends? She wanted to be friends with the man who had talked to her about Japanese glass fishing floats on a windy beach, not enemies with the restlessly angry doctor who sat before her now.

'I have been. . .had been. . .friends with Dr Thomas since I came here three years ago. He was getting ready to retire within the next few years, and was gradually handing his patients over to me. He was also planning to leave this practice to me in his will, but as you know he died five weeks ago, and at the time he hadn't made that will.'

'I see.' Karen nodded.

'I've been away, and when I got back last Monday I scarcely felt like contacting my old friend's lawyer immediately to find out when I could move into the surgery. It was only when he rang me this morning that I found out what Gloria had been up to.'

'Up to?' Karen questioned the loaded phrase, and Raiford Calvert's response was instant. 'She knew what Will intended—it was common knowledge here. You're a friend of hers, you must have known something about her affairs—and her husband's. You say you'd barely heard of Long——'

'But I'm not a friend of Gloria Denny's!' Karen exclaimed. 'At least. . . I like her, but——'

'You didn't know her in Texas?' he demanded.

'No. I've never been to Texas in my life.' Her English accent was very strong as she spoke.

'Then how on earth. . .?'

'I was here. . .well, on holiday, and I happened to see a notice in this window——' she gestured to her left '—saying the practice was for sale.'

'Yes, that's right,' Raiford nodded slowly, 'I remember getting the impression on the beach that you were a tourist. So you decided to up and buy it, and settle down here just like that.'

'Just like that,' Karen agreed. She didn't want to go into the story of the *Star of Scandinavia* going down, though no doubt he knew about it. But now that she would be living in the Long Beach area, she wanted to be known as Dr Karen Madigan, not as 'the girl from the shipwreck'.

'Then I guess you didn't know that Gloria wasn't at all happy about her father's decision,' Dr Calvert said now.

'No. I didn't know anything at all,' Karen said crisply. 'This is starting to sound like a television soap-opera. Are there any more startling revelations I should hear?'

She was feeling suddenly exhausted, and knew she badly needed some rest, and that she *didn't* need this kind of a scene. Her head was aching and her hands threatened to tremble. But of course he couldn't be expected to know any of that.

'I gather from your tone that you're not open to changing your mind?' Dr Calvert said.

'I haven't said that,' Karen replied wearily. 'I understand that this must be a big disappointment for you, but please don't ask me to make a decision now.'

'No, of course not,' Raiford Calvert said in a more gentle tone. 'That would be unfair. I'm sorry I've sprung this on you. I honestly assumed you knew far more than you did. Will you talk to Henry Sewell tomorrow?'

'All right.' Karen nodded.

She watched Raiford Calvert rise to his feet, but for the moment felt just too drained of energy to do the same. He must have noticed, because, without her fully realising what he intended to do, he was beside her and reaching down to take her arm in a warm, firm grip.

'Come on,' he said. 'You're tired. First day on the job is never easy.'

He pulled her to her feet and they stood facing each other only inches apart, his hand still holding her bare forearm. Again, as Karen stared at him, she was aware of what she had noticed on the beach—the well-moulded planes of his face, and those intelligent grey eyes. The intelligence made sense now. He was a doctor.

They stayed like that for what seemed like far too long to Karen, then he gently released her, his fingers sliding down so that they brushed her own as her arm dropped to her side. The awareness in both of them was unmistakable.

He broke the moment, turning away from her and saying lightly, 'Found any more fishing floats?'

'Not yet.' Karen's reply was equally light. 'I haven't had time for walks on the beach in the last few days.'

'No, I suppose you haven't. You certainly must have been busy.'

'Oh, Gloria did most of the cleaning out,' Karen said without thinking.

She saw him wince, and cursed her own insensitivity. Dr Thomas had been a close friend of his. It was scarcely tactful of her to remind him that all the old doctor's possessions were gone now. He was walking towards the door. Karen followed. He had opened it and was standing on the lower step outside before he spoke again. 'Well, I guess we'll talk soon.'

'Yes,' Karen agreed. She turned, closed the door, locked it and came down into the street as well.

'Goodbye,' Raif said.

'Bye.' She walked in the opposite direction down the road in the shafting late afternoon sun. There was a little red car parked about twenty yards off, and she was unlocking it and climbing into the driver's seat.

Raiford took a last covert look at her, then went round the corner to where he had left his own car. Driving away, he felt bad about the interview. He shouldn't have made so many assumptions, but on the other hand he did have strong feelings about all this. Gloria Denny hadn't impressed him on their two previous meetings. The way she had been eyeing off her father's assets had repelled Raif, although it always seemed clear that Bruce Denny, with his shady and unsuccessful business dealings, was behind it all.

Raif thought of his own father, and the way the man's repeated gambling debts and bad business moves had worn Raif's mother down. Alice Calvert was dead now, and Raif's father out of touch goodness knew where. Raif had tried to keep contact in spite of everything. Graham Calvert had Raif's address, but, in the three years since Raif had moved here, his father hadn't made use of it to send so much as a postcard.

Yes, there were some uncomfortable personal reminders involved in his feelings about the Dennys, and now he felt bad about the fact that he'd taken it out on Karen Madigan.

He swung his old blue Lincoln into a parking place outside Henry Sewell's office and almost jumped out of it before the engine had stopped running. He very much wanted to catch Henry before he left. Surely something could be sorted out that would leave both Dr Madigan and himself content. . .

'If the sale has gone too far. . .' Raif began, pacing around the lawyer's office.

'The sale *hasn't* gone too far,' Henry said slowly. 'You're very keen about this, aren't you, Raif?'

'It's what Will wanted as much as I did. I don't understand, Henry, I have to say, why you just let them go through with it. Why you didn't get in touch with me and give me the opportunity to better Dr Madigan's offer?'

'Because you couldn't have, Raif,' Henry Sewell said quietly. 'I'm your lawyer too, remember. I know enough about your finances. She's buying that place outright——'

'Outright?' I assumed. . .'

'You were hoping she was leasing the land and building and only paying outright for the practice itself?'

'Yes.' Raif sat down, then stood again. 'In that case. . .'

'If she agreed to back out, I could give you a week to arrange a loan,' Henry said.

Raiford shook his head. 'I've only just finished paying off my parents' debts. And I've got the mortgage on the house.'

'I thought so. That's why I didn't contact you, Raif. I thought you might try to raise the money and get yourself in over your head.'

Raif made a face. 'I don't think I've inherited that particular failing from my father,' he said. 'Sorry I've wasted your time. Tell Dr Madigan she can go ahead with my blessing.'

'There is one other possibility,' Henry said slowly. Raif turned away from the door—his hand had already been on the handle—came back, and the two men began to talk again.

Karen didn't even have to return to the car for a second load of luggage when she arrived at what turned out to be 25, Oyster Road. It was quite easy to carry all her worldly goods up to the cottage in one trip.

The place was as cosy and friendly as she had remembered, but somehow it seemed very bare when she had unpacked her clothing and the food items she was beginning to accumulate after two weeks cooking for herself at the Clambake Motel.

She had rented the cottage furnished, but a fridge and stove and semi-automatic washing-machine, a bed, rickety wardrobe and chest of drawers, two lounge chairs, two kitchen chairs and a small dining table provided only the barest practical sort of comfort. These things didn't make her new place into a home.

Ordinarily, Karen would have relished the task of imagining how she would transform the cottage with her own personal touches, but after today's difficulties, and with the legacy of fatigue from her spell in hospital, it all seemed too much. She didn't have a single pot, dish or utensil with which to cook herself a meal, she realised. That meant bread and cheese and tomato, or else a trip in the car for a take-away or a meal out.

Well, she wouldn't make that difficult decision now! Leaving the bag of kitchen supplies sitting in the middle of a bench, she wandered tiredly out to the balcony. Perhaps the sea breeze would help.

Below, the garden was overgrown, although someone in the past, either the absent owner or another tenant, had obviously made a good beginning. Gardening. . . Another task that Karen would normally have been keen about, but wasn't today. The next-door place was lush and beautiful, with a rich green lawn and a riot of different shrubs and flower-beds, many of which were starting to bloom. It looked like a lot of work.

There was no fence to border the next-door garden. Rather, the specially planted shrubs just gradually gave way to plants and grasses, which in turn were taken over by the grey-yellow sandhills that led to the pounding sea.

The sea. . . Karen lifted her face and felt the breeze cool her cheeks and move through her hair. Another comfort and stimulation, but again, because of her mood tonight, not enough. Suddenly she felt tears brimming uncontrollably and trickling their salty way down her face. Stupid to be crying! Necessary, though. She gave way to it, stifling sobs, but letting tears flow freely and wiping them away every now and then with the back of her hand.

'Dear? Excuse me. . .' For a moment, the woman's voice didn't penetrate, and when it did Karen assumed that the 'dear' was addressed to someone else. But it came again. 'Excuse me, dear, but I have to ask. . .'

Karen looked down. A woman was looking up at her from the next-door garden, hoe in hand.

'You sound so upset. Is there any way I can help?'

A worried frown beneath rather wild wavy grey hair was hidden as a hand came up to shade the woman's eyes from the glaring reflection of the setting sun on Karen's cottage windows.

'I'm so sorry,' Karen said stumblingly, regaining most of her control.

'Sorry? My lord, why should you be?' the woman exclaimed. 'You're the new tenant and you're upset, and I'm hoping I can help. I'm not about to report you for disturbing the peace with those tears!'

Karen smiled, then wiped her hand over her face again. Her eyes felt red and swollen, and her nose was about to drip most unbecomingly. As if guessing this imminent danger, the grey-haired woman pulled a folded wad of clean white tissues from the pocket of old crimson trousers, sat the tissues carefully on the metal end of the hoe and held it aloft by the handle.

Laughing, Karen bent down to retrieve them through the horizontal wooden rails of the balcony.

'You might have to brush the dirt off,' her resourceful neighbour said, lowering the hoe again.

'I scarcely need them,' Karen said. 'You've made me feel so much better already.'

Americans could be wonderfully friendly. Sometimes *too* friendly, but in this case Karen felt pure gratitude, and she sensed that she was going to like the wild-haired gardener with her cheerful brown eyes and energetically trim figure.

'Now, are you going to tell me what's wrong, or would you rather keep it to yourself?' she asked now.

'Oh, it's nothing really,' Karen answered.

'I'm Rosalie Thorne, by the way,' her neighbour put in.

'And I'm Karen Madigan. I've just taken over Dr Thomas's practice, and today was my first day, and I'm tired, and the cottage doesn't seem like home yet, and. . . Well, it doesn't sound very terrible, but that's why I'm crying.'

'My dear girl, it sounds like quite enough reason for tears,' Rosalie Thorne said, leaning emphatically on her hoe. 'You'll just have to come over and have a meal and spend the evening with us!'

So Karen did. At first she was reluctant and made excuses, but Mrs Thorne seemed so sincerely eager to welcome her that finally she felt it would be rude not to go. The evening was a delightful one in the end. Geoffrey Thorne was a successful Portland architect who was semi-retired now, and did most of his work in this coastal region of Washington. Rosalie was a weaver, and, with a family of grown-up children now scattered all over the western states of the USA, the Thornes seemed to have a very pleasant existence, pursuing their creative careers in a leisurely way in between visits to their children. A pleasant existence, and they were pleasant people as well—warm, widely read, free of small-minded attitudes.

When Karen looked at her watch and rose to leave, she was surprised to find it was ten o'clock. They had lingered all evening at the table over chicken casserole and salad, fruit and cheese, and mints and coffee, and her tiredness had vanished.

'A casual invitation, and now I've taken up your whole evening!' Karen said apologetically.

'Don't be silly, girl!' Geoff Thorne said. 'We love visitors blown in from distant shores.'

'*Literally* blown in!' Rosalie added.

Karen had found herself telling them much more about her life than she had intended, and they had been fascinated by her account of the shipwreck, and the strange impulse to stay on at Long Beach. One thing she did *not* tell them, however, was that Dr Raiford Calvert had already cast a doubt over her future in the area.

Fortified by the evening, and by the realisation that her neighbours were going to become good friends, Karen made up her new bed with far more cheerfulness than she would have thought possible a few hours ago. Nonetheless, it was of Raiford Calvert that she was thinking as she coaxed herself into much-needed sleep.

There were no patients at all the next afternoon, after she had spent the morning buying a basic collection of kitchen utensils, food items, and two potted plants to cheer up the small lounge-room. 'Surgery' was laughably similar to what it had been on Monday.

Karen wore her forest-green skirt and a cream blouse,

and realised that she'd have to shop for more clothes again very soon. She couldn't appear in a total of two outfits in front of Barbara, who was dressed in an attractive mauve today. Ridiculous to have to worry about saving face like that, but there it was. Her receptionist ought to be someone who she could make a free confession to about her current sparse wardrobe.

Again, Barbara sat at the reception desk all afternoon, and again Karen sat in the surgery catching up on medical reading. And what were those calls that did come in? She heard the phone ring at least six times, each time picked up very quickly by Barbara, but at the end of surgery hours Karen's casual question, 'Many appointments tomorrow?' brought the same response as it had done yesterday.

'Just one. I put it at two-thirty.'

'That's following the one that was booked yesterday for two o'clock?' Karen replied. It was half-statement, half-question, and her heart was thudding stupidly.

'No, that one cancelled,' Barbara said smoothly.

Somehow, Karen found that she had been expecting this news. She nodded, and after the same clipped goodbyes as they had exchanged yesterday, she left, Miss Stenlow having offered to lock up the surgery.

Henry Sewell, the lawyer. . . Karen had promised Raiford Calvert that she would see him, and she had telephoned to arrange it earlier in the day. The meeting wasn't a long one. He had a proposition to put to her, which she guessed he had worked out with Dr Calvert last night or this morning. Dr Calvert couldn't afford to buy the practice outright, it seemed, but he hoped that Dr Madigan would consider leasing it to him for the indefinite future.

The amount he offered sounded reasonable, perhaps even generous, but Karen's throat was tight as Mr Sewell left her alone in his office with coffee for a few moments to consider the offer.

'I can give you several days...' he had said, but Karen had replied that she would rather make an immediate decision. She was feeling tired and drained again, and it seemed as if she had had rather too many major decisions to make recently.

When Henry Sewell came back into the room again after ten minutes, she faced him firmly.

'I'm sorry. I can't accept the offer,' she said, adding quickly, 'It's not a matter of money. Offering more wouldn't help. But I've committed myself to staying in this area, and the practice, with the land and the building, is now tying up virtually all the savings I had.' She felt her voice fogging a little with held-back tears, then hardened it as she said almost self-mockingly, 'This might sound a little melodramatic, but I really have nowhere else to go.'

Being a lawyer, he didn't probe, but Karen saw him glance at her curiously and with a measure of sympathy.

'Very well,' he said. 'I'll tell Dr Calvert what you've decided.'

And that was that. Or so Karen thought then. A week later, she wasn't so sure. In many ways it hadn't been a bad week. She had expanded her wardrobe—it was lovely to have a whole collection of new things—and bought some framed prints to soften the bare walls of the cottage. An ochre-toned Indian rug now met her feet in the mornings when she stepped out of bed, and Rosalie Thorne had given her 'one of my early efforts'—another rug in soft hand-woven creams and beiges that didn't look like an early effort at all, and that made all the difference to the cool polished wood of the lounge-room floor.

Rosalie and Geoff had had her over for another meal as well, and the rest of her spare time had been spent swimming in the chilly but bracing ocean, walking on the beach, and just relaxing on the balcony with a book.

It was the practice that wasn't working out, and she was starting to lose badly needed sleep over it. She kept telling herself that appointments would pick up, word of mouth would spread that Dr Thomas's practice was back in action, summer people and tourists would arrive in greater numbers, people would stop staying away out of respect to Dr Thomas, but by Tuesday, a week after her meeting with Henry Sewell, numbers hadn't grown significantly at all.

She had been planning a full day's surgery hours this second week, but she hadn't needed Barbara to point out coolly that that seemed unnecessary, when she'd only seen two patients on Friday. Today, again, there were only two appointments scheduled, both early in the afternoon.

The first one was a disaster. She heard the ten-year-old boy's almost hysterical crying out in the street, and when he and his mother arrived in the waiting-room it became quite overpowering. Mrs Pagett's scolding and beseeching seemed to be completely ineffectual.

'Be quiet, Bradley! Will you stop that noise this minute! What would the other boys say if they could see you behaving like such a cry-baby. . .?'

The screaming did not diminish. Barbara opened the surgery door and said woodenly, 'Mrs Pagett and Bradley, Dr Madigan,' before ducking quickly back to the haven of the waiting-room.

Bradley was momentarily calm, while Mrs Pagett explained the reason for the visit. His face was red, his sandy hair a mess, and Karen could tell it was only a lull in the storm.

'He's going away to scout camp next month,' Mrs Pagett said, 'and they've asked all the boys to have mumps and measles immunisation. Apparently they had a measles outbreak last year. Of course we had the more serious diseases—polio and diphtheria, that kind of thing—done when he was little, but we never thought of mumps and measles as being dangerous.'

'Mostly they're not, of course,' Karen answered. 'But there is a rare degenerative disease that can follow the measles years later.'

'And I know boys can have a complication with mumps.'

'Yes, so since it's easy to immunise. . .' Karen stood up as she spoke and went to prepare the syringe and the necessary fluids. Immediately Bradley began to cry again, energetic crying that was more like a two-year-old's temper tantrum.

'Didn't you hear what the doctor said?' his mother pleaded desperately. 'You could get a degenerative disease, or you might be made sterile. You might never be able to have any children if you get the mumps.'

'The other boys said it hurts like hell. They said it hurts like stinking hell!' was the shouted, hysterical response.

Karen came towards him with her syringe and cotton swab of antiseptic. She guessed that to a ten-year-old the dim possibility of never becoming a father was of no concern at all, compared with the immediate promise of pain. She had come across nervous and frightened children before in her work, and it seemed as if the best thing to do was simply to continue calmly with what she had to do.

'If we could just have the sleeve of your T-shirt rolled up a bit more, Bradley,' she said to him, having to speak loudly to be heard above the piercing din of his voice. He was getting hoarse now.

'No!' he screamed, and when his mother tried to roll up the sleeve, he jerked and twisted out of her grasp. 'It's going to hurt like hell. It's going to hurt——'

'Bradley! *Bradley!*' Mrs Pagett barked desperately, but her son continued to writhe and twist so that Karen had to stand back with her syringe and swab out of fear of jabbing Bradley or his mother in the face. 'You are having this injection, son. . .'

'If you'd like to come back another——' Karen began tentatively.

'No,' Mrs Pagett shook her head quickly, 'I'm so sorry, Dr Madigan, this really is awful, but he has to learn that being scared beforehand only makes it worse.'

The struggling and screaming continued for several minutes, and then at last Mrs Pagett got a firmer grip on him and he went rigid, still screaming so that Karen's eardrums felt violently assaulted. She managed to swab his arm, then he almost strugged free again, with the desperate strength of a wild animal newly captured. By using one hand to help Mrs Pagett hold him still, and giving the injection awkwardly with the other, she finally managed to get the needle in, saying just as she did so, 'Bradley, if you move now it *will* hurt. *Badly!*' in such a firm, urgent tone that at the critical instant he was still.

It was a narrow thing, though. As soon as she had emptied the syringe and slid the needle free, he was jerking and writhing again, as if the procedure had been double the agony he was afraid of. But at least it was over.

'Thank you, Doctor,' Mrs Pagett said weakly.

Karen managed a nod and a smile. She wanted to tell the boy that it was his fear that had made the pain worse—his arm muscles had been so rigidly held that the needle had met with more resistance as it entered—but she simply could not face prolonging the interview. No doctor liked to be reminded of the fact that their work sometimes caused pain. Ushering them from the office, white-faced and having to conceal trembling in her limbs, she caught sight of Barbara Stenlow, apparently typing busily at her desk. Typing what? Karen asked herself. And she thought she saw a faint smile lurking about the woman's lips.

She'd be happy if I had that sort of trouble with every patient, Karen thought resentfully, then wondered if she was blowing this out of proportion.

As luck would have it, today's only other patient was already waiting. It was a girl in her early teens, accompanied by her mother. Both of them stared at Karen in her wilted state, and the young girl looked nervous.

If this one is going on a girl-scout camp, and all the other girls have told her that injections hurt like hell, Karen thought, I'm going home for the day!

Fortunately, she did not have to carry out this threat she had made to herself. The girl had come to have a couple of unsightly warts cauterised, and she was a model of ideal patient behaviour.

Nevertheless, by the end of the afternoon, the strain of sitting in her surgery and listening to the phone ringing intermittently outside, on top of the drawn-out saga of Bradley Pagett's immunisation, had become too much. Barbara always spoke softly into the receiver. Was it deliberate?

Karen got up, walked across the room and opened the door quickly and quietly.

'Yes, I can give you Dr Calvert's number,' she heard Miss Stenlow say, then she waited until the receiver was replaced.

'Miss Stenlow?'

Barbara turned around with a start, and redness crept quickly up her neck and on to her face. 'Yes?' she blurted.

'I'd like a cup of tea if you're not busy.'

'Of course.' Miss Stenlow glanced at her watch nervously. It was a quarter to four. Karen had never asked for tea this late in the afternoon before.

Karen returned to her desk and waited for her tea, thinking. No, she wouldn't confront Barbara. She was convinced that the older woman wasn't at the root of this. After all, what did she have to gain? No, it was Raiford Calvert, and she would make damned sure she saw him this afternoon. . .

His surgery wasn't nearly as prominent as she had expected it to be, Karen thought, as she climbed a flight of stairs to find a cream-painted door and a sign saying simply 'Dr Calvert's Surgery'. But it was certainly a thriving practice. Six people sat waiting in a small room, and the young blonde receptionist looked somewhat harassed.

'I've come to see Dr Calvert,' Karen said to her.

'Do you have an appointment?' came the automatic reply, at the same time as some hearty laughter from the surgery. Karen winced. Along with the large number of waiting patients, the cheerful atmosphere emanating from the next room only underlined the desolation of her own premises.

'I'm Dr Madigan,' Karen said shortly. 'I don't need treatment.'

'Oh, it's personal?' The girl opened her blue eyes widely. She looked like everyone's idea of a dumb bottle-blonde, but a medical receptionist needed brains, so no doubt she wasn't.

'Business,' Karen snapped back, disliking her own sharp tone but unable to help herself just at the moment.

'Well, there's no one else to come after this lot,' the girl said, gesturing at the six filled chairs. 'If you care to wait. . .'

'Yes, I will,' Karen said.

Fortunately there was a chair vacant in the far corner, next to the magazines. She buried herself quickly in a glossy women's weekly and took care not to look up each time Dr Calvert appeared in the surgery doorway asking for his next patient.

'Could I have that magazine when you've finished with it?' the woman next to Karen said after a while.

'Oh, yes, of course.' Karen smiled, looking up. She saw a rather red, weather-beaten face, framed by lanky dark hair. 'Please have it now. I've finished this article, and there are plenty of other things I can look at.'

'Need something to keep my mind off it,' the woman explained, gesturing with a movement of her head towards the surgery on the other side of the wall against which their chairs were placed. Evidently she was another nervous patient. Not Karen's own problem this time, but another reminder of Bradley Pagett. She winced again to think of how easily the needle might have slipped if he'd struggled at the wrong moment.

'Yes, it's always best to think about something else, isn't it?' Karen said in reply, aware that the woman's comment demanded a response. She hadn't actually looked at Karen yet, but was fiddling with the nervous fingers that rested in her lap. Karen saw an opportunity to sow some seeds of change in the woman's attitude, and added, 'It only makes the pain worse if you live through it ten times beforehand in your imagination.'

'Oh, it's not really the pain,' the woman said, tightening her arms around herself now, and hunching her shoulders. 'I just don't like—you know, hands on me.'

Again Karen nodded. She could understand the sense of personal violation that some people felt, especially women.

'I'm dying for a smoke,' her neighbour said. She had rather a horse, harsh voice, perhaps rasped raw through too many years of heavy smoking. 'But I should get called next, so I'd better not go out. It's selfish the way they don't let you smoke inside any more. It's an invasion of our rights, isn't it?'

Dr Calvert appeared in the doorway again at that moment, and said questioningly, 'Mrs Gill?' Thus Karen was saved from having to make the choice between dishonest agreement with Mrs Gill and defending her own view, which was that people should definitely *not* smoke in small enclosed rooms like this, particularly around other sick patients.

Mrs Gill got slowly to her feet. She must only be in her late forties, but her movements seemed to belong to someone of more advanced years. Then Karen saw that she was shaking, with tense, stiffened muscles, and that she was biting her thin bottom lip so that it had gone an almost greenish white.

She really *is* nervous, Karen thought.

It came as a surprise, then, when Mrs Gill came out of the surgery only a few moments later. After a brief word to the receptionist, she left the waiting-room, sprightly of step now, and able to give the door quite a triumphant pull behind her as it closed. She was already pulling a packet of cigarettes from her handbag. The whole thing seemed a bit odd, Karen decided, before returning to the magazine that Mrs Gill had never got around to borrowing from her.

It took over an hour for the waiting-room to clear. When Dr Calvert appeared at the door one final time, his receptionist didn't have time to speak. Karen put down her magazine and stood up, tall and slender.

'Dr Madigan. . .' Raiford Calvert said slowly.

'Hello, Dr Calvert.' Damn! She was wearing last Monday's burnt orange dress again, Karen realised at that moment. But most men didn't notice that kind of thing.

'She's been waiting a good while,' the blonde receptionist put in helpfully.

'Come in. . . You can go now, Stephanie.'

'Thanks, Raif.' The girl got up quickly and began to gather her things.

Karen was thinking, Raif? as she followed the doctor into his office. Rather informal.

'Now?' Dr Calvert turned to face her as soon as he'd shut the door behind him.

'You're sabotaging my practice!' Karen burst out.

CHAPTER FOUR

'THAT'S a very strong statement. . .' Raiford Calvert said slowly.

'Yes, it is,' Karen agreed.

They were both standing bristling and tense in the middle of his cramped surgery. Out of the corner of her eye, Karen took in a solid but not huge desk where today's patient files were still lined up, a screened operating table, some equipment, two upright chairs, little else. Cheerful striped curtains in the one window, though, and several quiet prints on the walls, as well as the inevitable eye chart.

'It's not true,' Dr Calvert said. 'But I expect I'll have to prove that somehow, and I only hope I can. I know what makes you think it.' He pulled the chair out from the wall. 'Sit down.'

Warily, Karen did so, and Raif took his place behind the desk. He wore a casual V-necked shirt of textured cream knit, and black trousers that fitted closely to his strong legs. The man did know how to wear clothes, although he wasn't an elaborate dresser. This was their third encounter, and Karen could picture each of his previous two outfits. Things like that didn't always stick in her memory.

She watched as he pressed fingers against eyes that were tired from a busy GP's day, then looked up at her. 'You've had patients call, find out about Will's death, and then ask for my number?'

'It seems that way, yes.' Karen nodded, a little surprised that he was being so frank about it. She had expected icy, hostile denial.

'Seems?' he queried.

'Miss Stenlow has taken the calls. I've been in the surgery. I haven't known what the calls were, but at the end of the day out of a dozen calls. . .more. . .there'll be one appointment. Even allowing for pharmaceutical representatives trying to sell me——'

'And you haven't discussed it with her?' he interrupted.

'She's made it fairly clear that she wouldn't welcome a discussion,' Karen said drily, 'even if it was about the weather.'

He raised well-drawn eyebrows, then was silent, frowning. Karen was goaded by this lack of a reply into rash words. 'And I've presumed—reasonably, I think—that you're behind it. That you've told her to encourage Dr Thomas's patients to go to you. It's clear that neither of you want me here. . .out of loyalty to him, or just spite, I don't know, and you've started this campaign. . . Well, I won't be squeezed out!'

'Just a minute!' He was angry now, and it seemed to darken his grey eyes so that they were almost black. 'Give me a chance.'

'Why? You didn't give *me* one the other day,' Karen flashed back. He ignored this.

'I'm not "behind" anything,' he said. 'There's something happening, clearly. I think I know what it is and I'll solve it for you. But you have to realise a few things. Have you ever had a general practice before?'

'No. . .'

'I thought not—you look too young. First, it takes a while in any new practice to establish yourself. . .'

'I do realise that, but the practice was already——'

'Dr Thomas had been gradually scaling down for two years. Henry Sewell told you that. The locals know it, and several of them haven't even bothered to ring his surgery since his death. They've come straight to me.

Other people. . . Well, it's always disconcerting to ring a Dr Thomas's number and find you've got on to a Dr Madigan instead.'

'Barbara could easily explain the situation and reassure people,' Karen put in hotly.

'Yes, she could.' There was something there that he had left unsaid, but Karen didn't stop to wonder what it was.

'You said you'd prove to me that you weren't deliberately poaching my patients. . .'

'I said I *hoped* I'd be able to,' he corrected her calmly. 'I haven't succeeded, evidently.'

'No. At least. . . I don't know whether you have or not,' Karen answered slowly.

'What are you going to do?' He was eyeing her narrowly.

'Try to find out from Miss Stenlow exactly what's happening during those calls,' she said. 'Other than that, I don't know.'

She got up, feeling a heaviness in her limbs, and a sense of defeat in her heart. He reached the door before her, holding it open silently. 'Thank you,' she said automatically as she passed him.

He reached out a hand and brushed her sleeve with his fingers. 'I'll talk to you soon.'

'Yes. . . Bye,' she answered, again without thinking.

It was only when she got outside that Karen wondered about his last words. She didn't particularly *want* to talk to him soon, but the Long Beach community was not an enormous one. He was probably right. They'd be bound to run into each other.

It was half-past five, and quite warm, although there was a curtain of haze towards the west that seemed to be building into cloud. Karen drove home quickly, feeling as if the encounter with Dr Calvert had achieved nothing.

Her anger and courage hadn't last after that first attacking statement. It was disconcerting the way he got straight to the heart of things and didn't fuel her anger by denial or counter-attack. Why should it be disconcerting? Surely his honesty should make things easier!

Irritably, she brushed aside these nagging questions, and decided that she'd ask the Thornes over for impromptu drinks. Her kitchen cupboards were well enough stocked now. But when she pulled into her driveway, she saw that the Thornes' carport was empty, and that Rosalie wasn't in her beloved garden, where she usually spent the late afternoon hours. The house looked closed up. . .and then Karen remembered that they had said on Saturday they were going to Portland for a few days.

She entered her cottage, restless and disappointed, and wandered on to the balcony. The sea breeze caught her hair and her dress, fresh and salty, and she knew she had to get out of the cottage again. Half an hour later, dressed in a casual skirt and loose blouse of the same sea-green as the ruined evening dress she'd worn on the night the ship went down, she was driving along the beach with both windows open, drinking in the blasts of air.

It felt good, even though the wind whipped tears into her eyes and chilled her ears. She'd never driven on the beach before, and in her heart she thought it was a pity that the local authorities allowed it—wheel-tracks, noise, oil splodges—but since it *was* allowed, and since other people did, she wanted to try the sensation of barrelling along the hard sand near the water's edge just once. The experience certainly suited her mood today.

Tomorrow, she had to face a difficult confrontation with Barbara Stenlow about those phone calls, still uncertain about Dr Calvert's part in the whole business. Just how would she bring up the matter?

She shouldn't have started thinking about it. Treading hard on the brake, Karen realised that she had driven way beyond the last vehicle exit from the beach before the prohibited area at Leadbetter Point. She hadn't been looking for it carefully enough. And now, on her windscreen, came the first spatterings of rain.

Without thinking, she swung the wheel to the right and started to turn back, taking it a little too fast. She skidded—not badly, but enough to make her heart lurch—and, by the time she'd recovered control, the car had buried itself up to the hubcaps in the soft sand higher up the beach and she was stuck.

Put it into reverse. . .press the pedal. . .cross fingers . . .swear. . .no, she was only digging the back wheels deeper in, that way. Forward again? Sand spewed out and she sank still further. She switched off the engine and got out of the car, tears of frustration at her own stupidity mingling with the tears caused by the wind. And it was really raining now, cooling the summer air down quickly so that her cotton skirt and blouse were very inadequate.

She took the keys from the ignition and set off down the beach. Why was it deserted like this? Because sensible holiday-makers had seen the rain coming and gone home, of course. She hadn't brought her bag, and didn't even have enough change on her for a phone call to a garage or tow-truck company. She'd have to find a sympathetic summer resident and ask to use their phone. The whole thing was an infuriating nuisance, specially since she had only herself to blame.

Usually alive to beauty, Karen was insensitive to the wild colours and planes of grey-ochre beach, grey-green sea, and rolling grey-purple clouds today. The first thing that caught her angry gaze was a long figure further down the beach, and, drenched to the skin now, she broke into a jog towards the stranger. This could mean rescue.

It wasn't a stranger. It was Raiford Calvert.

'Do you *live* on this beach?' she asked indignantly, when she saw that he had recognised her. He was dressed—sensibly!—in shiny black raincoat, black sou'wester, rolled-up grey trousers, and bare feet.

'I could ask you the same question,' he replied drily.

'I might have to live here in future,' she said grimly. 'My car's bogged back there. Look!'

He followed her pointing arm and saw the tiny red shape in the distance, then his eyes narrowed angrily. 'That's well beyond the Oysterville beach exit!'

'Yes, I know, I was——'

'Don't you realise you're supposed to keep well clear of the Leadbetter Point area between April and August? This business of beach access for cars disturbs me at the best of times, and perhaps a little thing like preserving the breeding grounds of an endangered bird doesn't seem important to you, but——'

'Listen, Raiford!' She faced him angrily. 'I do know about the Snowy Plover breeding area. I missed the exit by accident. I was trying to turn round to come back when I got stuck. Beach driving is legal. Perhaps it shouldn't be, but it is, and everyone else does it, so why shouldn't I?'

'"Everyone else does it!" has always struck me as one of the very worst reasons in the world for doing anything at all.' He had turned on his heel and was walking back along the beach.

She took several awkward skips after him, blurting desperately. 'Where are you going? Aren't you going to help me?'

'Of course I am. I've got a rope in the car.'

'Is it safe to leave my car. . .?'

He turned towards her and said with studied patience,

'It's not going anywhere, is it? If this was New York City, no doubt eight thugs would come along within five minutes and lift it bodily from where it lies, but out here...'

'I suppose so.' Karen laughed briefly at the graphic image he had painted, in spite of their recent anger, and saw him grin sideways at her.

It was really raining now, and windy too, and he seemed to take in for the first time the fact that she was very inadequately clad. A gust of wind twisted her drenched skirt around her legs suddenly and she tripped as it became too tight and clinging for her to take a proper stride. He caught her and steadied her, gripping her shoulders.

'Careful...'

Then he stopped and frowned, studying her narrowly. He hadn't let her go, although her balance was fine again now. He brushed a dripping wisp of blonde hair off her forehead, then traced a flowing line down over her shoulder and her back, stopping at her waist.

'You've had your hair cut,' he said softly.

'Yes, I... A month ago now, but...how did you know?'

For the first time since the shipwreck, Karen missed her hair—the comfort of its length and mass and weight, the hypnotic task of rhythmic brushing morning and night. But how could Raiford Calvert have known about those waist-length pale gold ropes? He'd murmured something, too, that she hadn't caught. A word beginning with 'm'.

'It's the colour of that skirt and the way it's all wet and twisted around you,' he was saying softly. 'You were on the *Star of Scandinavia* and I pulled you from the water.'

'You...!'

'You couldn't possibly remember it!'

'But I do. At least. . .' Karen pressed the heel of her hand against her wet forehead. 'There's an image. . .just a flash. . . I can't capture it at will.'

'You had a head injury, that's right.'

'I was unconscious for about ten days.'

'My God!' Raif exclaimed. 'Yes, we were afraid it might be quite serious. You're lucky to be——'

'I know,' said Karen quickly. Being a doctor herself, she didn't need to be reminded of how close her injuries had come to leaving a permanent legacy.

'You were white—almost blue with cold—that night,' he was saying now. 'And with your long hair, you looked very different. But you're tanned now, and thinner too, aren't you?'

'Yes, I'm afraid cruise ship food tended to. . .' She stopped. He still had a hand on her shoulder, and when she shivered he felt it and they both came back to reality.

'Come on,' he said, breaking into a rapid stride again and beginning to peel off his raincoat as he did so. 'You can't afford to be getting wet again like this. You're still virtually convalescent, and you're mad to be at work already. . .'

'No. . .' But it was only a faint protest.

The stiff plastic of the raincoat was scarcely comfortable pressed against the wet fabric of her blouse and skirt, with her chilly skin beneath, but it kept out the wind and soon her body warmth had begun to re-establish itself.

'Oh. . .!' she exclaimed suddenly.

He turned and grinned at the expression that had appeared on her face at the sight of his car. The large, rather dented old tank of a thing was scarcely what she was accustomed to in a doctor's vehicle.

'Something wrong?' he asked lightly.

'I'd have picked this as belonging to the eight thugs

from New York,' she answered, and was rewarded by a shout of laughter.

'It's only a question of priorities,' he said. 'This thing's much more reliable than it looks—as I hope you'll find when we rope your car—and reliability is all a doctor really needs in a vehicle.'

'True.'

'I prefer to spend my money on other things,' he elaborated.

'You don't think it could be a bad advertisement? People might think you were slapdash in your work...'

'Ah, back to the old question of what "everyone else" thinks and does.' It was a light comment, made as the car doors banged and he started the ignition, but it reminded Karen forcefully of his earlier anger, and she guessed that he was thinking of it too. It was a pity.

The realisation that it was he who had pulled her from the water and held her on the night the ship went down had softened the atmosphere between them, and had made her remember their second encounter too, when she had shown him the fishing float. Now she remembered their unresolved professional rivalry, and it didn't take much effort to work out that this was the more important element in their already complicated relationship.

And so they travelled in silence along the rutted track that led on to the beach and down to the hard reach of sand near the water's edge.

'Tide's on its way in,' was all Raif said before they reached the little red car. Karen felt uncomfortable at first, and searched her mind for small talk, but weariness was overtaking her now, and in the end she was happy to accept his verdict of silence.

He stopped safely down on the hard sand and they both got out to look at the stranded car. It looked worse than Karen had expected. Was that just the effect of the tiredness that was seeping deeper and deeper into her limbs? Raif walked around the car a couple of times, then stood and looked back at his own vehicle, clearly measuring and planning in his mind.

Karen followed him, sheep-like, feeling stupid because she had nothing to contribute and shiveringly aware of the trickle of icy rainwater running down the inside of her—or rather, his—raincoat collar.

'Well, you couldn't have done a more thorough job of it if you'd been trying,' was his frank comment as he went to the boot of his car to search out the tow-rope.

'Thanks!' Karen retorted.

'You're welcome.'

He took out the coil of orange nylon and lay on the sand under her back axle to attach it. 'You're pulling it out in reverse!' Karen squeaked when he emerged.

'Looked like the best way.'

He hadn't bothered to look at her, and was already striding to the driver's door of his own vehicle. If Karen hadn't been icy cold and turning blue she would have been flushing with impotent anger—not at him, not really. At the situation. She hated being thrust into the position of helpless female, and had changed many a tyre and poured many a pint of motor oil in her time, but towing a car out of boggy sand was, frankly, beyond her range of experience.

As if to confirm her uselessness, Raif wound down his window, leant on an elbow and spoke. 'Look, don't stand there getting wet. Go and sit in your car.' To be fair, it wasn't said unsympathetically, and then he added, 'I'll need you behind the wheel in a minute anyway.'

Karen nodded dumbly, and went obediently to her vehicle. Her legs were shaking. The temperature must have dropped at least fifteen degrees since she had left the cottage. She sat behind the wheel, watching raindrops chase each other down the sloping windscreen and not really paying attention to Raif's manoeuvres with his car.

When he tapped at her side window several minutes later, she wound it down and realised that the car had filled with the smell of wet fabric.

'OK, we're ready to go,' he said, bending towards her and almost needing to shout above the wind, which was gusting more and more strongly.

She took a quick look behind her and saw that the cars were now back to back, linked by as short a span of rope as Raif had felt he could get away with, without straying into the soft sand himself.

'Don't start your engine,' he instructed. 'In this stuff, you'd probably only plough yourself in deeper. Leave the car in neutral, and no handbrake, of course. Just concentrate on steering. Remember it'll be like the rudder on a boat. You'll have to swing the wheel in the opposite direction from the one you want the car to go in.'

'Just like driving in reverse gear,' Karen said.

'Yes, sorry... I made it sound unnecessarily complicated.'

'You were affected by the nautical setting,' Karen said, excusing him. She checked handbrake and gears.

'Here we go, then.'

He went back and started his car again, then began to pull. Karen could hear the labouring of his engine above the wind, caught the frightening creak and groan of the rope as it pulled taut, and felt her car shudder. It wasn't going to move. Raiford's engine wasn't enough... Yes, it was... It was free.

She held the steering-wheel carefully. This was when her task really began. He would keep towing until she was definitely safe on the hard sand, and perhaps as far as the Oysterville exit track, so that she didn't have any awkward manoeuvring to do to turn her car round.

Keeping the car straight was a little harder than Karen had expected it to be, and it took her full concentration, especially when he slowed to turn off the beach towards the exit track. She found that she had to brake a little to avoid catching up to him. She was glad the journey would soon be over...

But it wasn't over. He didn't stop.

'What on earth are you doing?' Karen said to him under her breath, but even if she'd shouted it, he wouldn't have heard.

The car was freezing, because with the engine off she didn't have any heating, and she wasn't yet completely used to the American way of driving on the right-hand side of the road either. Added to the fact that she was travelling backwards, with no control of her speed, and no idea of where they were going, it was scarcely surprising that her teeth were tightly clenched and her knuckles white where they gripped the wheel. Was this a kidnapping?

There weren't many cars about, fortunately, but there were some, and one of them narrowly escaped grazing the front bumper bar of her car as it passed on a cross street. He seemed to be slowing, but... She risked a look in her rear-view mirror. It was disconcerting. He seemed to be changing gear. They must have nearly crossed the peninsula by now. It was only a few miles wide.

'This is ridiculous!' Karen said aloud, and put on her brakes—gently at first, of course, then with increasing pressure.

Her car came to a halt and she then felt it jerked a little by Dr Calvert's heavier vehicle, which moved it on a couple of extra feet. She pulled on the handbrake to make sure. Raif was at her window within seconds.

'Thank God you did that!' It wasn't what she had

expected to hear, and when she turned to him, she found that he had gone distinctly pale.

'What happened?' She opened her door.

'I decided to pull you right off the beach to save you any difficult turns, then I remembered I'd forgotten to tell you to put your brakes on when you saw me slow down. I hoped you'd think of it. . .'

'I did.'

'Then I put on *my* brakes, and found they'd failed.'

'A reliable car, hey?'

'Till now. . .'

Suddenly they both laughed. It could have been dangerous, but they'd been lucky, and now it was safely over. Then Karen's laughter changed to shivering which she tried to disguise, but couldn't at all. The weather was building to storm proportions. Raif saw her wretchedness immediately.

'I think you'd better come inside,' he told her.

'Inside?'

'I live here in Oysterville. It's only a couple of hundred yards.'

'But Dr Calvert——'

'You're soaked,' he said.

'So are you.'

'I'm not recovering from a recent brush with death and a significant stint in hospital like you are,' he pointed out. 'You're coming inside, and what's more, you're staying to dinner. That cottage of yours'll be chilly and lonely in your present state.'

He seemed to know exactly where she lived, Karen noticed. Was Henry Sewell the informant? Raif was untying the rope from her back axle as he spoke, then he coiled it on his arm back to his car, undid it from his rear tow-bar, and dumped it in the boot.

I could just drive off. . . Karen thought. But she hadn't thanked him yet.

'Move over and I'll drive,' he said, returning.

Actually, the command came as a relief. She felt as miserable as a drowned rat and much more tired. She slid across to the passenger seat, narrowly avoiding bumping herself on the gearstick, and he climbed in and started the engine, apparently not needing to ask for instructions about how to drive this model.

If that was his car, Karen said to herself, thinking of the brakeless dark blue tank they had left parked on the shoulder of the road, what's his house going to be like?

She soon found out. A neatly trimmed hedge ran the length of the street frontage, then arched over a white picket gate. Inside, paving stones formed a curved path to the forest-green front door of a two-storey white-painted wooden house, with eaves and window-frames picked out in the same green. The front garden was not large but was laid out pleasingly with a lawn, several shrubs and a row of huge soughing pines. In the rain, the tips of their needles were misted with droplets of water.

Raiford Calvert ushered Karen in to a small vestibule, where a dark polished wooden staircase with a heavy, old-fashioned balustrade led up to the next floor. From the vestibule, they went forward into a roomy yet cosy sitting-room with bay windows on two sides, each containing a deep wooden window-seat scattered comfortably with cushions in plain bright colours like jewels—ruby, sapphire, emerald and amethyst.

Two woven cream wool rugs softened the polished wood floor; a forest of potted plants, including several Japanese bonsai, gave life and freshness; a fire was laid ready in the grey marble and green tiled fireplace; and piled in an enormous carved wooden bowl that was wide, shallow, and clearly of American Indian design, were at least half a dozen glass fishing floats of different greens and blues and browns.

'Hey,' Raiford said.

'Hmm? Raiford, this is such a lovely room!' Karen exclaimed, forgetting her cold wet limbs. 'Stunningly lovely!' She hadn't even looked at the prints and paintings on the walls yet.

'Hey!' repeated Raiford. 'Will you please get upstairs and into the bathroom? And take a long, long shower—only leave me a bit of hot water.'

'Then what. . .?' The idea sounded so warming and wonderful that she didn't want to protest, but what would she wear afterwards?

'There's a cupboard in there with big towels, and I'll get you some clothes.'

Five minutes later she was standing under a gush of steaming water as warmth gradually returned. There was a knock at the door and Raiford Calvert's hand dropped a pile of clothes on to the clean tiled floor with a soft plop, then he was gone again.

When Karen came down the stairs a while afterwards, she felt almost respectable in the white cotton T-shirt, cream cashmere sweater, maroon silk pyjama pants and matching maroon silk dressing-gown.

Had he bought those silk things for himself? Karen wondered idly, then it came to her with a slight shock that she had seen no sign of a female presence in this lovely place. Clearly, he wasn't married. Was there no woman in his life at all? That was difficult to believe. He had a good profession, and he was certainly attractive. . .

She brought herself up short. Squash that thought out of existence at once, Karen Madigan! It had been all right to think it that first day on the beach when he had been an anonymous beachcomber like herself, but it wasn't all right to think it now! The rival medical practices were still a huge, unresolved issue between them. In a sense they were enemies. What on earth was she doing in his house—and wearing what amounted to little more than silk pyjamas?

Perhaps it was lucky he wasn't in the sitting-room when she re-entered it. He *had* been there, though, while she was in the shower, and had been busy. The fire was lit, and crackled with orange sparks and flames, throwing a glow on the glass floats and tinting the white-painted walls a golden yellow.

He had drawn heavy dark green curtains across the windows, turned on two wall-lamps shaded with fringed silk, and opened a bottle of wine which looked a mellow ruby-red in the warm light. She could hear sounds coming from the kitchen and wondered whether she should offer some help. No doubt it would be something quick and easy. Lasagne or quiche, perhaps, bought frozen from the supermarket and heated in a microwave.

She could hear the lash of rain and wind in the gathering darkness outside. Maybe it wouldn't hurt if she just stretched out her fingers to the fire for a moment. . .

A gentle hand on her shoulder woke her, how much later, she didn't know. 'Dr Madigan?'

Karen opened her eyes slowly and saw Raif bending towards her, his face half shadow, half glow from the firelight. 'Shouldn't you be calling me Karen by now?' she queried lazily. It seemed absurd—asleep on his hearthrug, dressed in his clothes and being addressed so formally. She had relaxed totally while asleep, and the question of anyone's medical practice had become somehow unimportant.

'Sure. And for you. . . Most people call me Raif.'

'Raif,' she echoed. 'Nice.'

'Slick, I'm told by a few people.'

'Brisk, certainly.' She summoned the energy to sit up.

He had poured the wine, and handed her a long-stemmed glass. On the hearth, well within reach of the heat from the fire, sat a thick black iron pot filled with a rich soup, almost a stew, of seafood swimming in a sauce of tomato and garlic, herbs and wine.

'Hungry?' he asked. 'Like seafood?'

'*Like* it!' Karen was suddenly aware that she had an appetite as sharp as a knife.

'I know with seafood the wine should be white,' he said. 'But red always feel so much warmer, and after today...'

But that shivering hour on the beach seemed to belong to another life.

'I'm as warm as toast,' Karen said, feeling the heat tightening the skin on her face. 'And starving!'

He pulled a plate of fresh oysters garnished with slices of lemon on to the rug, and taking stock of her immediate surroundings Karen saw that there was a round loaf of crusty wholemeal bread, and a green salad tossed with herbs and French dressing as well. There was more. Further back, out of reach of the fire's heat, sat two bowls of fresh berries, a mixture of red, crimson and bluish purple, cream in a small jug, and a bottle of mineral waster in case the glorious tastes needed the contrast of some plain liquid. Raif had brought the cushions from the window-seats over too, so they could loll comfortably on the floor by the fire as they ate.

'Have I been asleep for three hours?' Karen asked, disbelieving.

'More like three quarters of an hour.'

'So you have meals like this just waiting around for when you rescue people off rainy beaches?'

He laughed. 'I like cooking, I have a friend who runs an oyster lease, and I made the bouillabaisse this morning, planning to eat some tonight and freeze the rest for another day. I'll still do that. We won't get through all this.'

'You don't know how hungry I am,' Karen threatened.

'Yes, and you need to cover those elegant bones a little more thickly,' he drawled.

They began with the oysters and lemon.

'To be honest,' Karen said, 'after your car. . .'

'I think I know what's coming. . .'

'I expected a tin shack, a packet of soup, and tap water.'

'Didn't I tell you before?' he responded lightly. 'It's a question of priorities.'

'Well, you've got them sorted out *almost* perfectly!'

'I think I might be forced to do something about the car, yes. . .'

It was a long, lazy and utterly wonderful meal. The wine was good, the music on the compact disc player soft and mellow, their conversation interesting yet undemanding, open but not threateningly personal.

'What's the time?' Karen asked lazily when she had reluctantly pushed aside the empty berry bowl.

'Getting on for half-past ten.'

'That late?'

'No need to get up yet.'

They were both stretched on the rug now, almost touching.

'The clearing-up?' she protested.

'That can wait,' he said. 'Listen, I've been thinking. . .'

'Hm?'

'About the practice. . . No, don't stiffen up like that.'

Karen had. She tried to relax again, and almost succeeded. His warm bare foot, gently nudging her own, helped considerably. Raif went on.

'There's a very easy solution. We go into partnership. I've got too many patients at the moment, and you've got too few. My surgery's too small—as I'm sure you saw today. Yours. . . I know Will had that big spare room just getting cluttered with medical junk. . .'

His voice, with its surprisingly mild American accent, was low and steady, and what he said made a huge amount of sense. Now he had stopped speaking and was watching her, his eyes a cool dark grey and his mouth firm-lipped. He didn't seem to be waiting for an instant response.

Karen thought about how she had lain awake last night staring into the darkness and tossing back and forth, worrying about the whole business with Barbara Stenlow and the lack of appointments. How long could she keep going with almost no money coming in? A month at the very most, discounting a loan or an overdraft.

If she had to sell, how long would it take to find another buyer? If she left Long Beach, where would she go? What did she have in her life now to propel her in any one direction? Back to England? Yes, she had friends there, but they were all married now, and rapidly becoming absorbed in questions of London versus country, skiing in Switzerland versus cruising in Greece, career versus full-time motherhood, breast- versus bottle-feeding. . .

Where did she, out of sheer circumstance so rootless, fit in? Perhaps, way back two years ago, the cruise ship job had been the wrong choice?

At three o'clock in the morning, these questions had loomed very black indeed. Now here was Dr Raiford Calvert, lying lazily beside her in the glow of a warm fire, offering her answers to all these dilemmas on a plate. Wasn't she mad to be even hesitating? It seemed that way.

'I like the idea. . . I think,' she said slowly.

'Karen! I was really holding my breath.'

'Thought you looked a bit blue.'

They smiled at each other, then suddenly the thing

that had been inevitable all evening. . .inevitable, perhaps, since the man on the beach talking about glass fishing floats had re-entered her life as Dr Calvert. . .happened. They had rolled together on the warm woollen rug and were in each other's arms.

His kisses tasted of strawberries and raspberries and blueberries and cream, and they seemed to go on forever, sometimes gentle, sometimes firm and hungry, always slow and tender and alive to her own response. His hands, too, seemed to understand her body straight away. Those limbs and curves which, earlier in the evening, he had said were not full enough, seemed to soften and melt under his touch until they throbbed with awareness and pleasure.

He kissed the lobes of her ears, the curve of her neck, and the dent in the middle of her collarbones. He wound his arm around her so that she was cradled in his warmth and surrounded by the musky scent of his aftershave. She felt the hard press of his torso and thighs, a contrast to the softness of his hands and mouth. . .

It was getting dangerous. There was absolutely no reason for it to stop at all, and the rational part of her didn't want that continuation. Far too soon. Far too sudden. Karen Madigan had a good mind, and she didn't ever let it get talked down by the contradictory demands of her body. This felt so right now—it *was* right as far as it had gone—but if it went any further, she would regret it, heavily and thoroughly, for a long time.

'Raif. . .'

As if sensing her need to withdraw, he released her with a last lazy caress that sent a tingle, a rippling wave of tingles, running all down her body.

'Want to help me take all this into the kitchen?'

'Yes, of course.'

It was a very effective dousing, and if Karen hadn't been convinced that it was necessary, she would have been bruised by it. The kitchen was cold. And Raif started talking about practical matters again almost at once.

'There's quite a bit to discuss, of course,' he said.

'I'm sorry?' said Karen, confused.

'About the partnership.' He began to stack the dirty dishes on the sink.

'Oh, right.' It was the last thing she felt like thinking about right now, although his proposal had set her mind at rest about a lot of things tonight.

'Not now, of course,' he went on.

'No.' Karen glimpsed a kitchen clock on top of the fridge. A quarter to twelve. Which meant that the time they had spent in each other's arms must have been——

'I'd better call a taxi for you,' he interrupted her thought.

'A taxi?'

'I'm not suggesting you've drunk too much, but you're dog-tired, I can see it in your face, in spite of that nap by the fire. Better sleep in tomorrow.'

'I will.'

'And I'll drop your car off at the surgery for you, shall I?'

'Mmm, fine.'

He went into the entrance hall and picked up the phone, and she could half hear his voice speaking into it. She returned to the sitting-room and brought out some more dishes, put them on the sink and then turned away, wondering what else she could do while she waited.

It was a spacious, old-fashioned kitchen, with a wooden dresser and a big wooden table that looked comfortably worn from use. A large piece of thick paper lay on the table, next to a bowl of bright fruit, and Karen studied it curiously. It was a drawing. No, a sketch, or not even that. Just a few flowing lines in water-colour forming an abstract shape of pale lemon cream and deep burnt orange.

Raif came back. 'On its way,' he reported briefly.

'Do you paint?' Karen turned to him impulsively.

'A bit.' It was abrupt and dismissive, and she felt shut out suddenly. He'd done it deliberately, and yet it had been an innocent question, hadn't it?

He was running hot water noisily into the sink and clattering the dishes almost violently. Karen caught his heavy frown and set mouth, and did not dare to speak. In a single moment, the flavour of the evening had been spoiled, and when she heard the taxi outside ten minutes later she felt only relief.

CHAPTER FIVE

KAREN stirred and looked at the travelling-alarm by her bed. Eleven o'clock. It couldn't be that late, could it? The bright light seeping through her curtains told her that it was. Her head felt heavy and throbbing and her mouth was as dry as dust. She had slept almost too soundly, and her limbs still felt drugged with it.

What was she wearing? She pulled the bedclothes aside. Raiford Calvert's white T-shirt and maroon silk pyjama pants.

She got out of bed and padded off to the shower, blinking the sleep out of her eyes, and thinking about the end of the evening. She'd dropped straight into bed as soon as she arrived at the cottage, and that had been her mistake. Why hadn't she drunk some of the mineral water at Raif's, or poured herself a glass when she got home? Or at least changed out of these clothes of his, that smelled faintly of a lemony laundry detergent.

Raif. . . It all looked different this morning, and she mistrusted last night gravely. Didn't it have all the elements of a classic seduction scene? Lulling her by warming and feeding her so well after their earlier adventure, and then taking advantage of her when all her defences were down. . .

Only the object of it all hadn't been to get her into bed. Raiford Calvert had had a more long-term and practical goal in mind—the medical partnership. What was more, Karen had agreed to the idea. It was not a binding agreement of course, but she knew, and flushed hotly at the realisation, that she would not dare to go back on what they had decided. That would be a complete betrayal of how successful his seduction technique had been. She had to convince him that, in the cold light of day, the proposition looked just as good to her as it had looked when he held her in his arms.

After a light brunch of fruit and bread and tea, Karen dressed in a stone-white linen suit, with straight skirt and cardigan jacket over a white silk blouse, and walked to work to clear her head, arriving only just before one. Surprisingly, the surgery was still dark and locked. Barbara usually came at half-past twelve.

There were two messages on the machine, both requests for appointments this afternoon, and for a brief moment Karen's heart lifted. If business suddenly picked up, she could legitimately claim that she and Raif didn't need to form a partnership. But then good sense reasserted itself. One swallow—or two sore throats—didn't make a summer.

When Barbara arrived fifteen minutes later, it was clear that she had been crying. Her face was ugly and puffy, making her look older than her forty years. Was it a family problem?

'Is there anything wrong? Can I help?' Karen asked as Barbara took off the pink silk scarf that had been tied over her hair.

'Oh, no, it's just hay-fever. I've been sneezing all morning,' Barbara answered awkwardly, with a poor attempt at brightness.

Clearly it wasn't the truth, but everyone was entitled to a protective lie of that kind at one time or another. Karen nodded, manufactured a remark about high pollen count, and didn't push any further. She was about to disappear into her surgery to follow the afternoon's usual dreary pattern of silent medical reading, punctuated by the ring of the telephone and the sporadic appearance of a patient, when Miss Stenlow pulled her back with some words.

'Oh, Dr Madigan...'

'Yes?'

'Here are your car keys. Dr Calvert gave them to me and said he'd parked your car just down the road.'

Karen's heart lurched at the sound of his name, and she was ashamed at her unwilling reaction. She saw that Barbara was stifling a curiosity about the car, but she was definitely not going to make an explanation to the older woman about the events of last night. Barbara would just have to stay curious. But there was another element in Miss Stenlow's emotions, and in a sudden flash of intuition Karen decided that it was Raiford Calvert who was responsible for the unsightly red eyes, blotched eye-liner and swollen nose.

At that moment, the telephone rang, and Barbara turned to it with a gulp, composing her features carefully. 'Dr Madigan's surgery.'

Karen listened shamelessly, inventing an errand among the patient files in the top drawer of a cabinet behind the reception desk.

'Yes, the practice is running exactly as it was before,' Barbara was saying carefully. 'Dr Madigan will be able to look at all Dr Thomas's notes about your previous visits, and I'm sure you'll find her very satisfactory... An appointment this afternoon, then? At four o'clock? Yes, we can fit you in at that time.'

Karen shut the file drawer and went into the surgery. When three more appointments were booked in for that afternoon, she knew that her intuition had been right. Barbara Stenlow had received her orders from Dr Calvert: no more deliberate turning away of patients.

The confrontation in his surgery yesterday seemed to have been worthwhile after all. Or perhaps it was their dinner together that had caused the change. And yet did any of it really matter? If they were going into partnership together, her desperate grab for patients no longer counted, and Dr Calvert's talk with Barbara was an empty gesture. . .

None the less, after an afternoon of sketchily described stomach pains, a child's fever, an infected toe, an annual check-up, and other sundries, she decided that such a routine series of ailments had never been so satisfying to treat as they had been today.

Half a dozen appointments dotted over the four-hour surgery period scarcely amounted to a hectic day, but after a week and a half of regal solitude among her medical journals, it was at least a taste of real medicine again.

At four o'clock, Karen thought she had finished for the day, and she was a little surprised to hear Barabara's too-discreet tap at the door.

'Can you see someone else?' Miss Stenlow asked, leaning into the room but blocking the slightly opened door with her body so that the patient in the waiting-room could not see or hear. 'She doesn't have an appointment. . .'

'Well, I was planning to stay until five, as usual,' Karen said. 'So it's no trouble. Is it one of Dr Thomas's patients?'

'Yes, it is. I'll bring in her file. Mrs Gill,' Barbara said, then retreated from the room and shut the door before Karen could register any surprise.

Mrs Gill! That was the patient whom she had sat next to, only yesterday—it seemed longer ago than that—in Dr Calvert's waiting-room. Surely he wasn't going to start returning Dr Thomas's patients to her when they'd already shown up for an appointment with himself? She was still trying to piece the story together when Mrs Gill entered.

'This is all my damned husband's idea,' she began, before Karen had even been able to say hello. 'I don't need a check-up.'

It appeared that Mrs Gill had no recollection of sitting next to her in the waiting-room at Dr Calvert's. Still, that happened to everyone at some time or other. It could be difficult to recognise someone whom you had just chatted to for a moment, if you encountered them next time in a very different role.

'Do sit down, Mrs Gill,' Karen said, sounding very English. 'Just a general check-up, or was there something specific you thought I should look at? Anything that's worrying you?'

She thought it best to stay calm and businesslike, and not address the question of Mrs Gill's husband. Was this going to be another difficult patient? It seemed that way.

'I've told him I hate to come to doctors, but he won't take any notice. He's in the car waiting outside, and he says if I come out too soon he's going to march me right back in again. But there's nothing wrong with me.'

'I'm sure there isn't,' Karen began, trying not to be distracted by wondering why Mrs Gill had come here instead of to Dr Calvert. It felt like something she should be angry about. In their new partnership would he, with his greater knowledge of the people in the area, palm *all* the difficult patients on to her? She continued quickly, reining in her wandering thoughts, 'But it's a good idea to have a check-up every year or two so that nothing has a chance to develop unnoticed. For example——'

'I suppose he told you I smoke and drink too much,' Mrs Gill butted in, as if she had heard none of Karen's reasonable words.

'Your husband hasn't told me anything,' Karen said.

'Not Jack, Dr Calvert I'm talking about.'

'Oh, did he——?' Karen began. Again Mrs Gill interrupted.

'I went to see him yesterday and he said how he knew I got nervous and he thought I might be more at home with a woman. I don't think it'll make a bit of difference, but I didn't tell him that. I just agreed so I could get out of his office.'

Betraying this deception didn't seem to worry Mrs Gill. She got to her feet and started to roam the surgery nervously. 'I wish I could have a smoke,' she said, just as she had done yesterday. 'And a drink. Jack and I always have a gin and tonic at four. I should have put my foot down and not come.'

Karen, seeing herself about to go through a longer, subtler version of yesterday's scene with Bradley Pagett, seized on a desperate idea. 'Mrs Gill,' she said, 'if you sit and have a cigarette and a drink now, will that help you to get through an examination without being too nervous?'

'Oh, would it ever! But I wouldn't be allowed to smoke here. . .' she added craftily.

'Well, as it happens, since you're the last patient of the day, I can make an exception just this once,' Karen said.

She felt guilty as she poured a small glass of brandy for Mrs Gill. It came from a bottle of good-quality French stuff that she had found when she took over the practice. She wasn't sure if Dr Thomas had kept it for his own use or for the very occasional patient who might need some unorthodox calming method. As long as her little trick worked, it would be all right, but if Mrs Gill left the surgery with brandy on her breath and billows of smoke in her wake, having again refused to be examined, Barbara Stenlow might have something to say. And you couldn't hold down a grown woman the way Mrs Pagett had held down Bradley.

Mrs Gill chatted quite amiably as she drew on her strongly flavoured cigarette and sipped at the brandy and water. It seemed likely that she was verging on alcoholism as well as smoking too heavily, but Karen decided that she had to win a degree of confidence and relaxation from Mrs Gill if she was to get any chance at all to attack these long-term problems.

She began the examination while the last half-inch of brandy and water was still in the glass. Easy things first—eye chart, a simple audio test, reflexes, pulse and blood-pressure. The last two were not quite what they ideally should have been. When she asked Mrs Gill to lift the striped polyester blouse she was wearing, and pressed the cold circle of the stethoscope to different parts of her back in turn, she felt the older woman begin to stiffen with nerves and reluctance, but nothing was said.

'Just breathe nice and deeply for me,' Karen said, listening to the stethoscope's amplified message.

Mrs Gill's breathing remained too shallow and there came the distinct bubbling, rasping sound of congestion and restriction in her lungs.

'Have you had any pain in your chest at all? Any pain when breathing?'

'No, none. My family have always been as strong as oxen. There's nothing wrong with me!'

Not the right time to point out that emphysema was probably on its way, even if it did take a number of years to develop. Certainly not the right time to mention the possibility of lung cancer.

'Would you just pop into the next room and put on a gown now, Mrs Gill?' Karen said. 'You'll find a clean one already in there hanging on the peg, and there's a bench and more pegs to put your own clothes on.'

This was the difficult moment. Would Mrs Gill refuse? Karen held her breath, then let it out again carefully as Mrs Gill got to her feet slowly, with a deep sigh but without protest. She came back a few minutes later, dressed in the gown but with circles of nervous perspiration already darkening its pale blue beneath her arms.

When Mrs Gill was lying on the paper sheet that

covered the lightly padded examination table, Karen gently moved each front flap of the gown aside while she performed a breast examination, rotating the tips of her fingers in small circles around the whole area. No lumps or abnormalities of any kind, thank goodness.

Next came the most invasive test of all. By warming the plastic speculum in hot water before taking it out of its sterile cellophane pack, moistening her gloved hand with a transparent, non-greasy gel and pressing her other hand firmly and gently on Mrs Gill's abdomen first to relax the muscles, Karen was able to take the tiny cell sample which was so important in detecting cervical cancer early. A small electric cooling fan over near the window gave a soothing whirr in the background. The building had warmed up by this time, in the afternoon sun.

'You can get dressed now, Mrs Gill.'

'Is that it, then?' The woman seemed incredulous.

'Just some questions still to ask.'

'Questions! I hope it's only questions.'

'It is, I promise,' Karen said, as she prepared the glass slide for sending to the pathology lab.

Mrs Gill disappeared into the changing-room again, still subdued and quiet. When she returned, her belligerent manner seemed to have returned as well. 'So what are these questions?'

Karen asked her about diet, exercise, other ailments or illnesses in the past, or any unpleasant symptoms in the present, and created a picture for herself of a woman whose naturally strong constitution had thus far allowed her to escape the consequences of treating her body badly.

'And just before you go,' she said finally, opening a lower drawer in her desk, 'here are some pamphlets that might help you to stop smoking.'

'I don't want to stop smoking,' Mrs Gill snapped back.

'I've had this check-up because Jack wouldn't have left me alone if I hadn't, but I'll kill myself in my own way and in my own good time, thank you. You doctors, interfering in my life, trying to take away all my pleasures because you say they're bad for me. I'm not coming again, you know. You're as bad as any man!'

She had left the room before Karen was able to reply. Despondently, she went over to the windows and opened them to their full extent to try and get rid of the lingering odour of cigarette ash, then she rinsed out the brandy glass and put the bottle safely away. It didn't seem as if that 'treat' in the beginning had achieved anything. What was the point in an examination if the patient refused to follow up on the results by improving her lifestyle?

'I thought I'd win her over, but I didn't,' Karen said to herself aloud. It felt like failure.

When the intercom buzzed at five, she answered almost mechanically, 'Yes, Miss Stenlow?' Another late patient?

'Dr Calvert is here to see you.'

'Send him in,' Karen replied lightly, but her stomach had dropped. 'Barbara gave me the car keys,' she said defensively when he entered, energetic in navy blue trousers and a paler blue shirt that made his grey eyes seem very cool and steady.

'Yes. I didn't know if I'd catch you before you finished to give them to you personally,' he said.

'Sit down.' She gestured towards the upright chair that sat at right angles to her desk.

He did so, casting a casual eye around the room as if to look for changes she might have made to Dr Thomas's set-up. In fact, she'd made vitrtually none. But he frowned and wrinkled his nose.

'Is that cigarette smoke? You don't smoke in your surgery, do you, surely?'

'I don't smoke at all,' she countered quickly. 'I let

Mrs Gill have a cigarette in here. Not something I plan to make a habit of, but she seemed so nervous and resistant——' She broke off and then added coolly, 'Are you intending to hand *all* the difficult patients over to me?'

The tart question vented some of the doubt and hostility she was feeling about last night, and Raif had the grace to look guilty.

'Was she very bad? I'm sorry, I didn't know her husband would bring her to you so soon.'

'I think you need to explain a bit further.'

'I intend to,' he said lightly, choosing to ignore the barbs in her tone. 'She had been Dr Thomas's patient for a long time, and she's always been very difficult. . . Won't take any advice about her health and has a lot of fear about being examined. Did you get her to have a pap smear and a breast check?'

'Yes, I did.'

'Then you've done very well. Will and I had talked about sending her to Janine Griffith. She practices in Grays River, which is quite a drive, but she's good. Then when Mrs Gill came in to me yesterday I suddenly thought she should try you, and from the sound of it things did go better. . .'

'So perhaps softening her up with brandy and a cigarette *did* achieve something,' Karen said drily, and saw him raise his eyebrows. Her shrug quickly made it clear that this wasn't something she would do with Mrs Gill again, even if it had been a success this time.

'But I intended to tell you all about her before she came in. Sorry it didn't work out that way. She's an ongoing problem, I'm afraid, but perhaps we'll find a better way to deal with it in partnership. . . Which, of course, is why I've come.'

He leaned forward energetically in his chair, his strong jaw jutting above the even colour of his tanned neck.

Evidently the subject of Mrs Gill was closed for the time being, and Karen decided she didn't have any more to say about it anyway.

'So, how soon do you think we can get this thing going?'

The confident directness of the words angered her suddenly. Typically American! she told herself, wilfully disregarding her own American blood. Brash, insensitive, assuming that everything was just fine and dandy. But if she wasn't prepared to renege on yesterday's cosy fireside decision, what was the sense in protesting? No sense in it at all.

'As soon as you like.' She forced herself to speak calmly, without meeting his gaze or echoing his dynamic attitude. 'I thought it over carefully this morning.' Not really the truth. 'It seems to be clearly the best solution for all concerned.'

The triumphant glint in his eye was quickly masked, but not quite quickly enough.

'Of course, if we find it's not working,' Karen blurted, defensive again in an instant.

'I'll only be paying you a monthly rate,' he answered smoothly. 'It won't be a difficult relationship to dissolve.'

Karen slumped in her chair and closed her eyes for a moment, not caring what he thought. The only thing her life seemed to consist of these days was making arrangements, signing papers, revising those arrangements. She wished that, just for once, she didn't have to be so *responsible*!

She opened her eyes again. Raif was standing above her, frowning. He reached down and touched her shoulder lightly, with stretched fingers.

'OK?' he said.

'Yes,' she nodded, 'just wishing I could be a child again for a while, that's all. No decisions, no signatures, no bills to pay. . .'

'I know the feeling.' He laughed, taking his hand away and pressing it against the back of his neck, just where the dark hair softened into some small curls above his tanned skin. It was an odd gesture, an uncomfortable one, making his elbow stick out sharply, as if he was embarrassed and holding himself back in some way.

Only last night they had kissed for a long and satisfying time, but today that memory seemed to belong to two different people, not themselves. There was no awareness in his grey eyes when they met her own green ones. No, in fact they *didn't* meet her gaze, they skated away.

Perhaps, Karen found herself thinking quite coolly, he was a little ashamed of himself for using seduction to get what he wanted as a professional. She hardened her jaw. So he should be! She blocked out the humiliation and regret that she could very easily have felt. It was an incident. It was in the past. She was mature enough to salvage a working relationship with him, since it was necessary.

'I had no idea my small surgery had so much in it,' Raif said as he stood among piles of bulging boxes in the previously empty room where Dr Thomas had stored a lifetime of old medical journals. 'Let's do the pictures first, shall we?'

'Pictures?' Karen echoed blankly.

He had arrived with a small rental truck an hour ago and she had helped him unload dutifully, but without much spirit. It was a warm Saturday summer morning, ten days after their agreement had been reached. There was a finality and a reality to it all now which had Karen feeling hemmed in, not to say trapped.

They had printed stationery—envelopes and paper in different sizes—they had prepared a new entry for next year's telephone directory, and they had even sent out a form letter to every one of Dr Calvert and Dr Thomas's regular patients, informing them of the change.

I should have been doing all these things three weeks ago, instead of just reading medical articles while I waited for the phone to ring, Karen realised, forgetting the state of weariness and dislocation that had inhibited her back then.

Raiford Calvert's powers of organisation were formidable. It shouldn't have come as a surprise. Any man who could prepare a three-course meal in an hour, for eating by an open fire, was clearly far from slap-dash, but somehow the speed and smoothness of all this made her uneasy. Just how far ahead had he planned? And now he was talking to her about pictures.

'I thought we ought to take them all down off the walls, and out of this box, and start again,' he was saying. 'Give the whole place a fresh flavour. It's a new era. Will wouldn't thank us for keeping every instrument and every chair in the same place as he had it. And I think your surgery needs a little more decoration.'

'Oh, you do?'

In fact, she had taken down one of the prints—a rather sugary landscape which had irritated her with its mass-produced look during that first painful week. He'd found that print now, leaning face to the wall in this bare room where she had guiltily placed it one day after Barbara had gone home.

'This, for instance,' he was saying, flourishing it in the air. 'Which I frankly loathe. . . What's more, it was a gift from someone Will heartily disliked. But the long wall in your surgery needs something.'

He was observant. Clearly he remembered the print from its previous position.

'Actually, there's the most gorgeous water-colour in the waiting-room,' Karen confessed. 'I'd been wondering before if I could steal it for my surgery without Barbara noticing.'

He had begun to disarm her again with his honesty about the landscape print, and with the fact that his tastes seemed to coincide with her own. Actually, he had a history of disarming her far too easily. . .

'What?' he responded, not laughing at her confession as Karen had expected him to.

'The seascape,' she said.

'Oh, that, yes.'

'If you'd like it in here. . .'

'No, you have it.' He was frowning and had closed off somehow, in a way that she didn't understand. She felt a tingling in her temples as the muscles around her face tightened with tension.

She was being a fool, an absolute fool. For a moment she'd felt as if they were two newlyweds discussing the décor of their new home, when in fact they were merely business partners, and it had to stay that way if things were going to work out for her here at Long Beach.

Raif hadn't kissed her since that night by the fire in his house. He hadn't made the smallest attempt to, and he hadn't asked her out. Oh, they had had coffee together twice, but that was purely in the course of organising their partnership. It didn't matter, Karen told herself, not for the first time. She didn't want their working relationship complicated by a romance. Absolutely not.

Why, then, did she feel this burning disappointment when he remained at a perfect, proper distance? The answer was painfully clear.

I will *not* fall in love with him! The words drummed fiercely in her head, and it was an effort to speak aloud. 'Let's not spend too long over the pictures,' she said very firmly. 'I'd like to be out of here by lunchtime if I could. If you can manage to set up your surgery on your own.'

'Yes, of course.' He leaned down and ripped a piece of strong plastic tape off one of the cartons.

Karen watched his hands as he first pulled the cardboard flaps open, then went to the next box and ripped the tape from that one in an identical gesture. She was already angry with herself again. For a fleeting instant, she had tricked herself into reading disappointment into that 'of course'.

'Perhaps the pictures should wait, then,' he said, after quite a long pause. 'I hadn't realised you wanted to go. There's something else we have to discuss.'

'Yes?'

He straightened, still holding a piece of buff-coloured tape in his firm fingers. 'We haven't faced the question of what to do about Barbara and Stephanie. We should have done, but I've been putting it off.'

'I'd assumed. . . Is there a problem?' Karen asked stupidly.

'In one building, we don't need two receptionists.'

'No,' agreed Karen. 'You hadn't said anything. I assumed Stephanie wanted to find another job.'

'Unfortunately, no. In fact, she very much wants to stay.'

There was a silence, and Karen felt him watching her. Barbara had been only a little easier to get on with over the past ten days. She no longer encouraged patients to go to Dr Calvert, but she certainly didn't extend any warmth or friendship towards Karen. With the new partnership looming, Karen had put her worries about the receptionist out of her mind. When Raif arrived, surely Miss Stenlow would behave more pleasantly. She was just the type who didn't enjoy working for another woman, that was all. But now it seemed there was a competition between the two receptionists, and either Barbara or Stephanie would have to go.

'I want to ask Miss Stenlow to leave,' Raif said slowly now.

Karen shot him a questioning glance. She had very much expected him to offer Barbara the position, for Will's sake as well as for practical reasons.

'Isn't Barbara far more experienced?' she said, sounding as if she herself was arguing for Barbara to remain. 'She's been on these premises with Dr Thomas for fifteen years.'

Raif frowned and opened his mouth to speak, just as the door behind him squeaked on its hinges and a mellow summer draught swept into the room. Barbara herself stood there, looking flushed, and dressed in one of her work outfits—a rather severe crimson suit. She carried a neat white envelope in her hand.

'Thank you, Dr Madigan,' she said. 'But there's no need for you to argue in my favour.' She held out the envelope. 'This is my resignation. I've found employment with an old friend of Dr Thomas's in Ilwaco—Dr Fred Rebbeck. I'm sure you know him, Dr Calvert. I'll be starting there in two weeks, and in the meantime I thought I'd take a small holiday and visit my sister in San Francisco. So, since it appears Stephanie wants to stay. . .'

'Yes, she does.' Raif nodded again. 'That's very convenient, then.'

'Of course, I've very much enjoyed working with you, Dr Madigan. . .'

Karen managed to smile, then started a little as Raif almost snatched the envelope out of Barbara Stenlow's hand with a murmured word. The latter seemed unnerved by the abruptness of his gesture too, and she concealed a frightened gasp behind a dry cough, then brought a neat pale handkerchief to her nose.

'I think I'm getting a cold,' she said.

'Better get home to bed, then,' Raif said shortly. 'Thank you, Barbara.'

'Yes, Dr Calvert. Goodbye.'

Barbara left awkwardly, ushered out of the building in very deliberate fashion by Raif. He slammed the door of his new surgery behind him as he re-entered, and Karen jumped, then almost shivered as she saw his set jaw and blazing eyes.

'I don't understand women like that,' he rasped, pacing the room, then finishing up in front of Karen, with hands gripping her shoulders till they ached. 'What does she have to gain? What kind of distorted shrine to Will's memory has she set up inside herself?'

'I don't——' Karen began.

'No,' he answered for her, 'you don't know what's been going on. And you don't know, you have no idea, how refreshing that is to me! That you're not the kind of person who goes in for those games!'

'Raif. . .'

'She's taken every opportunity to bad-mouth you behind your back. . . Oh, I know she's stopped doing it over the phone in surgery hours. I managed to get that under control for you last week. But she was born in this area and she knows a lot of people There's been some damage done.'

His hard grip had softened now, and his hands slid round her back to form a loose embrace. Karen felt his warmth seep into her skin through the thin silky blouse she wore, and longed to respond with her own fingers, exploring the trim tapering of his waist, but she made herself stay still and unresponsive.

'You could have stood back and watched it happen,' she said carefully, needing to know more from him about what he felt. 'Bided your time until I had no choice but to leave.'

'Yes, I could have. Originally, you thought I was

actually behind it,' he said. 'No, I can't stand that sort of thing. I'm pretty blunt myself. If I want something, I ask for it, or I go for it, openly. Barbara's lonely. She was in love with Will, or thought she was. She must have gone on hoping he'd marry her long after she should have seen that he didn't notice her in that way at all. Now she'll be working for Dr Rebbeck, also a widower, and about five years younger than Will. I wish her joy...' He shrugged, a bitter gesture, and Karen murmured her thought without stopping to censor it.

'It upsets you more than it should.'

He shrugged again, defensively this time. 'I cared about Will. She thinks she's been doing this for his sake, but as far as I'm concerned she's muddying his memory. His death shouldn't have led to that kind of underhand behaviour.'

'If I hadn't washed up here...'

'Literally!'

'Literally or not. If I hadn't decided to buy this practice...'

'You had a perfect right to. You've got your own life, your own priorities to struggle with.'

'That's not what you felt at first.'

'I told you—when I want something, I go for it openly. Wasn't that what I did?' He touched her lightly under the chin and grinned down at her.

'Hmm.'

'Didn't I?' he insisted. 'I barged in here and told you to get out of town, like a sheriff in a cheap western, but when I found out it wouldn't help me to get what I wanted... Well, I simply changed my goals.'

That was the moment when Karen knew she should have turned away, out of the arms that were softening and curving fully around her now, but she didn't. Instead, when he coaxed her gently forward, she responded and met his lips with her own in a kiss that instantly brought back all the longings and satisfactions of that night eleven days ago when the fire's warmth had heated their passions.

His lips felt familiar, yet with all the heady danger of new responses created in her every moment. How could lips do this? How could it feel so right, yet so unexpected? It seemed that she had to stay in his arms for hours in order to find out.

'When I want something, I go for it openly,' he had said. Didn't that mean she had been wrong in all those fears and suspicions about their seductive evening by the fire? There had been no hidden motivation there, no attempt to manipulate her through the response of her senses. He simply wanted the same thing that she did. . .

When his hands strayed up from where they had been caressing the rounded shapes of her hips and found the naked V where her blouse was open at the neck, she thought he was about to coax the buttons undone, and she knew she wanted this too, and wanted to feel his smooth warm palms cupping and moulding her tingling breasts.

Instead, he just touched her lightly there, and moved his hands up still further to caress the slim line of her jaw.

He spoke. 'Didn't you want to leave by lunchtime?'

'Oh. . .perhaps it won't hurt if I stay,' she murmured weakly.

'We do have a lot to do. . .' he said.

'Yes.'

He released her and her skin was immediately chilled, the fine blonde hair on her arms standing on end, although it was a warm day. 'I think we were talking about the pictures, and you wanted the seascape from the waiting-room.'

'Only if——'

'Don't make a fuss! It's fine.'

'Thanks. I'll move it now, then, shall I?'

Her response was deliberately as brief and clipped as his own, but just as she had taken a step towards the door she felt his fingers on her elbow and heard his murmured, 'Hey. . .'

She turned to him questioningly.

'I'm sorry. It's all right,' he said.

It was after three by the time Karen left, and Raif was still there, unpacking his case files and medical equipment. In only a few hours, they had changed the whole feel of the place, moving pictures and rearranging the waiting-room so that patients had a better view from the window.

'We should plant a bed of shrubs and flowers in front there, don't you think?' Raif had said, and again it felt as if they were setting up a house together. This time, Karen had let herself feel that way, and she decided it was nice.

In her own surgery, Raif had had suggestions to make. 'Not better, just different.'

'Better, I think,' Karen had responded.

The proportions of the room and its contents seemed more harmonious now, and she could look up from her desk and see that water-colour seascape, lit softly and naturally from the window. It reminded her of the thing she loved most about Long Beach Peninsula, the sea.

Gathering her bag when finally there was nothing more she could usefully do, Karen knew that she was watiing for Raif to kiss her again, and she heard her, 'Goodbye, then,' come out on a thin, half-questioning note, which she was sure he would interpret with ease.

But he only straightened from the pile of books he had just dumped on his desk and smiled, a heart-stopping smile that made crinkly fans at the corners of his cool grey eyes. 'Yes, see you Monday,' was all he said.

'I can make do with a smile like that,' Karen told

herself as she tapped down the three steps in her low-heeled cream leather shoes.

'See you Monday,' echoed in her head. She had almost hoped he would suggest dinner tonight, or something tomorrow. A picnic. Clam digging. Sightseeing. She hadn't visited the Cape Disappointment lighthouse yet, or the Lewis and Clark museum. Still, as with his smile, Monday would do. . .

By Monday, Karen had developed a cold. Not just a common cold, a real humdinger of a cold. It had started to overtake her on Sunday night, she had slept lightly, fitfully and feverishly, and by Monday morning it was fully fledged—dripping nose, stuffy head, raging throat, violently aching limbs and erratic temperature.

Struggling into the surgery by nine, she wondered how she would make it through the day. Raif, there already, didn't leave her in doubt for very long.

'Back to bed!' It was clearly an order, and she obeyed it gratefully, getting up during the day only to prepare herself hot drinks of soup or lemon and honey, and then again at five when the doorbell rang. It might be Rosalie Thorne from next door. . .

It was Raiford.

'House call,' he teased briefly.

'I'm following orders, Doctor, I promise,' Karen managed in return, then quickly brought a tissue to her nose again. It was red and sore by this time, and with hair straggling and tangled from a day spent tossing against rumpled pillows, she must look a sight. She *wasn't* glad he had come!

She shivered in the breeze from the open doorway, and he stepped inside, shutting the door behind him.

'I'll give you another order, then,' he said, pressing her gently in the small of her back so that she had no choice but to lead the way back to her untidy bed. 'Take the rest of the week off.'

'But——'

'No buts! You're run down, and that's what's let this germ get hold of you.'

He walked ahead of her and arrived at the bed first, quickly plumping up pillows and smoothing out sheet and blanket so that it was an inviting place once more. Karen sank gratefully into the mattress, and murmured weakly, 'I'll be better by Wednesday. It's my first week in the new partnership.'

'You've never allowed yourself a proper convalescence after your injury, Karen,' he said firmly.

'I did. I took——'

'From what I can gather, you took two weeks in which you rearranged your entire life, including buying a medical practice and a car. Since then——'

'Oh, Raif,' she sighed gustily, letting go at last. 'You're right. If I could stay in bed all week. . . If you could manage without me. . .'

She sneezed several times, and coughed some raspy, barking coughs which felt as if they were lacerating her scratchy throat. Her whole body ached. For an answer, he simply bent down and kissed her lightly but unhurriedly on her hot forehead. Karen let her eyes drift shut, and by the time he had let himself quietly out of the house she was asleep.

CHAPTER SIX

'IF YOU could call the surgery next week, the results of the test should be in, Mrs Delancey,' Karen said pleasantly. 'There wasn't anything else you wanted to see me about, was there?'

'No, just the regular annual smear,' answered Jenny Delancey. 'I don't know why I always ruin the sunniest month of the year by having it in August. I should come in December.'

'And spoil Christmas?' The young woman laughed, then Karen added, 'But seriously, do you find the procedure so very bad?'

'The worst part is my imagination,' Jenny Delancey confessed, brushing an over-long auburn fringe out of her brown eyes. 'I live it through a dozen times before I get to the surgery, then after it's over, I wonder why I wasted the time torturing myself.'

'At least you don't let that silly fear stop you from having the test at all,' Karen said, thinking of Mrs Gill's problems in that and other areas. 'Unfortunately, a lot of women still do.'

'Yes, I must talk to my sister about it.' The recently married redhead nodded. 'I know she puts it off. "I'm only twenty-five," she keeps saying.'

'Cervical cancer doesn't take a lot of notice of age,' Karen said.

'So. . . I'll call next week, then,' Jenny Delancey finished, standing up and collecting her bag.

As soon as she had gone, Karen pressed the intercom buzzer. 'Who's next, Stephanie? Claire Koslowski?'

This was the name on the file in front of her. Stephanie

was capable and thorough, and rarely did she fail to arrange the afternoon patients' files in order on Karen's desk at lunchtime.

'No, she hasn't turned up, Karen,' came Stephanie's bright, bubbly voice through the intercom. 'Mr Greenidge is waiting, though. Shall I send him in?'

'Yes, do, thanks.' Karen shuffled the files.

Harry Greenidge's was three files further down. He'd arrived very early. Karen had barely any time to flick through the thick wad of notes before the rather weather-beaten man in his mid-fifties entered the room. She saw that there were some pages in what she had come to know as Dr Thomas's crabbed handwriting, and then several more in Raiford Calvert's clearer hand. Mr Greenidge must have been one of the first patients that Dr Thomas passed on to his planned successor.

If she had seen that the file was so thick before responding to Stephanie's question, Karen would have asked for a few minutes alone to check it all through. Evidently the man had a complicated medical history.

'How are you, Mr Greenidge?' she said neutrally when he had seated himself with a grunt in the stiff-backed chair.

'I'm not feeling too good at all,' he answered in the slow drawl of a country-bred man.

He was dressed shabbily, like an outdoor labourer, though Karen glanced down at the file and saw 'Occupation: Clerk, Grant's Hardwear', listed below his address and birth-date. She also saw repeated question marks beside lists of hazy complaints, written with firm quotation marks around them.

In Dr Thomas's and, later, Dr Calvert's opinions, the man was clearly a malingerer. Karen, taking in his tired, puffy eyes and lack-lustre manner, wondered if there was more to it than that, and when he started listing his symptoms in a clumsy, worried sort of way, she noted each of them down meticulously.

'I've also come about this,' he finished, holding out an index finger and pulling off a piece of grubby bandage as he spoke.

The finger was red and swollen, around an imperfectly healed cut, and beneath the skin there was a yellowish colour in some parts.

'I think it's got a bit infected,' he confessed ruefully. 'I should have looked after it a little better, I guess. Cut it a week ago, out fishing.'

Karen shuddered inwardly, seeing in her mind's eye a clear picture of a dirty fishing knife and some rough and ready first-aid.

'It certainly is infected,' she said, preparing to lance it and drain off the unpleasant liquid beneath the skin. Then she prescribed an antibiotic as well as an antiseptic powder, and sent Mr Greenidge on his way with instructions to return early next week, partly because of the infected cut, but more because she wanted a chance to consider his other symptoms more thoroughly.

When he had gone, she buzzed through to Stephanie. 'Don't send the next patient in just yet, will you?'

'OK, when you're ready,' came Stephanie's ever-cheerful tone.

She really did look like a 'ditz', as the slangy American word went—a dizzy blonde. In fact, she was diligent, alert and always friendly, with an intelligence that would make her an asset to any practice, and a repartee that had Dr Calvert in chuckles several times a day.

Karen took her finger off the intercom switch, sat back in her chair and studied Harry Greenidge's notes again. She had come up with a diagnosis that seemed to fit, but it wasn't a pleasant one, and she wanted to make sure. Cancer of the colon. Not fun. Should she schedule a colonoscopy? It was the obvious next step. . . Two pages back in his notes, she found that he'd had one only three months ago and it had been perfectly clear. Raiford Calvert's handwriting and the typed report left no doubt.

Well, it was good news, but it left Karen confused, and she began to understand the irritation that came clearly through both previous doctors' terse clinical observations. Those same symptoms Harry Greenidge had described again today—feeling off-colour, not enjoying his food, nausea, bowels not working in the same way they used to, a general fatigue and malaise that he didn't even have the words for.

'Do I believe you, Mr Greenidge?' Karen said softly aloud. 'Or do you just hate your job?' She honestly didn't know. Perhaps it was something to discuss with Raif tonight. They were having dinner together, the second Friday night in a row.

After the last patient had departed two hours later, Karen again allowed herself some moments alone at her desk, but for a different reason this time. She stretched happily, flinging her arms back towards the window, which let warm sunlight flood in and on to her back, through the square-shouldered summer print dress she wore.

It was August now, traditionally a month of windy storms alternating with warm, pleasant days in this region, and today was one of the latter kind. Her cold had been gone for two weeks, and the weariness and persistent stress she had felt for so long before that seemed to have burnt itself out with the aching fever and congestion that had kept her in bed for the whole of Raiford's prescribed week, and into the weekend beyond.

She felt as if the medical partnership was established now. Raif was still the doctor most in demand, but all except a few die-hard old-timers were happy to be passed on to Karen's care if Dr Calvert was booked up, so her days were almost as busy as his now. It looked as if the Ocean Park practice was going to be a popular one. What was more, she was starting to love the work. It was her first real experience of general practice, and she found the human element of it so interesting. The way people reacted to illness was just as fascinating as the illness itself, and her understanding of human psychology was tested daily by the stream of patients that passed through the surgery.

She and Raif were getting on very well together too, and Karen was relaxed and content about it. It looked quite likely that a business relationship would blossom into romance, and it seemed almost amusing now to think back on the various flare-ups they had had earlier on. He was taking it slowly, but Karen didn't question that.

They both needed to consider their feelings very carefully, because there was nothing more dangerous and destructive than a brief affair turned sour and finished with, when the two people involved had to go on working together afterwards. They both needed to be pretty sure that they knew where they wanted it to go *before* they got properly involved.

Where they wanted it to go. . . Karen thought, almost complacently, that she was starting to have a good idea about that.

When Raif knocked at her surgery door half an hour later, then opened it and appeared there, smiling, she allowed a wide, answering smile to light up her face.

'Feel like a walk on the beach to build up our appetites before we eat?' he asked casually.

'Mmm, lovely.' She nodded. 'I was going to change, though.'

She brushed the skirt of her floral print dress as she stood up, and he swept his eyes over her briefly, with a slight frown, before saying offhandedly, 'No, you look fine.'

'It's just an office dress——'

'No, really. Fresh. . . I like the colours. Those splashes of different pinks and greens. So many women seem to wear black all the time at the moment.' He was gazing into the middle distance as he spoke, and frowning heavily.

'All right, then. I'll just wash my hands.'

Karen went out to the small bathroom. After a busy day in the surgery, she needed to splash her face and reapply her light make-up as well. Raif had sounded a little absent and distant just then, but she shut her mind to any worry. You couldn't poke and prod obsessively at everything a man said, in search of darkly sinister hidden meanings.

It was perfect on the beach. Karen held her ivory leather sandals in one hand and splashed barefoot beside Raif through foaming water that washed in and teased at their ankles, then ebbed again to reveal glistening sands. The sun hung over the sea, a burnished golden ball, sinking slowly and painting scarves of high cloud more and more brightly every minute. It was neither too hot nor too cool. . .

Almost perfect. Three four-wheel-drive vehicles zoomed past them on the hard sloping sand. The last one veered towards the water, its driver daring the waves and sending up an arc of water that splashed Karen's dress with sand and salt. Without apology, perhaps without even realising that he had wet her, the driver accelerated to overtake one of his companions.

'Are you still in favour of driving on the beach?' Raif asked drily, sweeping back a lock of dark hair that had been caught by the wind as he faced Karen.

'That's outrageously unfair, Raif!' she retorted, only half joking. 'I was never "in favour" of it. I tried it once to see where the thrill lay, and now I'm on your side. I don't think cars belong here.'

He shrugged, smiled briefly as if he thought she was over-reacting to his challenging question, then picked up a smooth silvery piece of driftwood and threw it at the water. They kept walking in silence. Raif seemed to be holding something back today, and Karen wondered if the evening was going to be the relaxing few hours she had expected and hoped for.

They were trying a new seafood restaurant further down the peninsula in Seaview—nothing elaborate, just a modest place where there was a softly lit bar and some cosy booths around the walls. Raif suggested white wine with their meal rather than a cocktail at the bar beforehand, and Karen was happy to agree.

The ocean air blowing on to the beach had sharpened her appetite and made her mouth water at the very thought of oysters. She had them deep-fried and coated in seasoned breadcrumbs, with wedges of lemon and a small pot of tartare sauce, along with salad and French fries, and following a creamy bowl of clam chowder. Raif chose his oysters natural to begin the meal, and followed them with fresh salmon in a herb sauce. The place was full and the level of conversation around them slowly rose as they continued their meal.

Karen noticed a red-faced middle-aged man at the next table laughing loudly and sitting back in his seat so that an ample paunch shook freely, and she was reminded for some reason of Harry Greenidge's visit to the surgery that day. She leaned forward and broke a small silence. Raif had started on his salmon, and she had just finished the second of her plump, succulent oysters.

'I wondered if you could give me any help with Mr Greenidge,' she said.

'Help?' He frowned.

'Yes,' said Karen. 'I'm getting mixed signals. He's got a file this thick.' She gestured with finger and thumb. 'His symptoms suggest cancer of the colon, but the colonoscopy you scheduled came up clear. He seems genuinely worried about feeling ill and not having an illness he can put a name to, but you and Dr Thomas have been sceptical in the past.'

'Sceptical?' Raif snorted. 'The man's an out-and-out fraud! Will came across him when he first started practising in this area. Harry Greenidge dropped out of a heavy-duty engineering degree halfway through and has been a clerk at Grant's Hardware ever since.'

'I'm sorry. . . Is that significant?' Karen had wondered herself if the man might be trying to get out of work that he found tedious and boring, but she wanted to play devil's advocate at the moment. There was something about Harry Greenidge that was sending out warning bells. She thought of the way his skin had seemed to hang loosely on his jowls, and remembered the old belt pulled in tight at the waist to hold up trousers of quite a large size.

'He's lost weight, hasn't he?' she said now, not waiting for Raif to answer her previous question.

'Yes, he has, now that you come to mention it.' Raif nodded slowly. 'I was in the waiting-room as he was leaving and I noticed it. His wife must have got him on a better diet at last. He's lived on meat and potatoes and eggs and bacon and beer for most of his life, and I told him at his last visit he needed more fibre and fruit and vegetables. As to his college career and his job—he had the intelligence to be more than a hardware clerk and he didn't make use of it. He's been playing truant from life ever since. They never had children, although there was no medical reason why they couldn't have, they still rent the same run-down cottage they moved into when they married, and never bothered with the garden. . . It's just a jungle of weeds and grasses. He's simply idled his life away fishing, and, when the salmon's running, he suddenly develops a bad back or a migraine. Doesn't stop him from going out in a boat, just from standing behind a counter.'

'It couldn't be a case of the boy who cried, "Wolf," could it?' Karen suggested. 'You've got so much into the habit of thinking he's making it up. . .'

'If so, I still don't think the wolf has shown up,' Raif said. 'That test was clear, remember? So were a couple of others we had done. We've tried everything we should have tried. He asked to see you today, knowing you were new. Doesn't that suggest that he knows he can't fool me any longer?'

'Yes, perhaps it does,' Karen admitted reluctantly.

What he said made sense. She was new in the region and less experienced in general practice, where, as she had been thinking only this afternoon, a hefty slice of human psychology that couldn't be learnt from textbooks was an essential requirement of the job. She didn't want to be one of those keen young doctors who saw a career-advancing crusade in every unusual case. No doubt Raif was right, and if she rushed Harry Greenidge all over the place for expensive tests, when several of them had been done already, she would only make a fool of herself.

Raif shifted restlessly in his seat. 'Do we have to talk about work?'

Karen refocused her attention, a little surprised at the impatience behind the words.

'Of course not,' she said. 'I just wanted your opinion. Perhaps I should have left it till Monday. . .?'

'No.' He seemed to realise that he had been unnecessarily abrupt, and reached out a hand to touch hers lightly across the table.

Karen responded to the gesture with a smile and the press of her own fingers on the sculpted back of his hand. It was dry and warm, tanned and just a little roughened—probably from gardening and from the scouring of the sea breeze during those long and frequent walks of his along the beach.

She started to explore its shape caressingly, but then he pulled the hand away, frowning, and leaving her groping on the table-top, and embarrassed about the betrayal. Her cheeks burned and she took refuge in a too-large gulp of wine that stung her throat and threatened to make her splutter.

Why was the evening going wrong? Or was it only that she had, without realising it, been looking forward to it far too much, and had been counting on it to give her a clear indication of where their relationship might be going?

His voice brought her out of this unsatisfying reverie. 'So. . .if I object to talking about work, it must be up to me to think of an alternative topic, is that right?' It was a gentle question.

'It seems fair,' Karen responded, taking her cue from his light tone.

'The summer's nearly over, but you've been so busy with one thing and another, I doubt you've seen as much as you ought to of our region.'

'No, I haven't,' Karen answered. 'You've decided on tourism as our topic, have you?'

He laughed, fortunately failing to detect the slightly bitter note in Karen's words, which she regretted as soon as she'd let it creep in.

'I was going to propose tourism as an activity,' he was saying. 'It looks as if the weather will stay on our side tomorrow. How about a tour of the lighthouses and the Lewis and Clark museum, with a picnic lunch?'

'That sounds lovely, Raif.'

Warmth flooded her again. This meant something, surely! Those moments of tension earlier. . . Well, you had to allow a busy doctor some tetchiness at the end of a long working week. Talk came easily to both of them for the rest of the meal. The subject, of all things, was fishing. Raif told her about the huge salmon runs of the old days, the thickly populated clam beds, and the shifting fortunes of the oyster trade in Willapa Bay.

Clearly, he hadn't treated his move to this community casually, and must have acquired more knowledge than many old-timers about its history, and the history of the Chinook Indians who had lived here for thousands of years before white settlement.

Karen was still listening to him, shining-eyed and leaning forward in her seat, when they finished their dessert of cream-topped apple pie, accompanied by aromatic coffee.

'I'd better take you home before I put you to sleep right here at the table,' he said finally, as their empty plates and cups were taken away by a soft-footed waitress.

'No, it's been fascinating,' Karen said. 'Just the right introduction to tomorrow's picnic.'

As he drove her back to Ocean Park, they talked about practical matters—the food each of them would bring, what time he would pick her up, and what was the likelihood of rain. Then a silence fell as they turned into her street, and Karen chided herself inwardly when she found that she was wondering whether he would see her to the door, and whether he would kiss her.

His words came as a disappointment. 'I'll wait here till you're safely inside.' He hadn't turned off the engine either, and was drumming the tips of his fingers lightly on the steering-wheel, as if impatient to get this goodnight out of the way with no awkwardness and no fuss.

'Don't worry,' Karen said. 'I've got my key right here, and the lights are on next door at the Thornes'. I'm quite safe.'

He nodded. 'See you tomorrow, then.'

'Yes, at half-past ten, as we said. Goodnight.'

She was out of the car already, and closed the door quickly and quietly behind her. He had pulled away from the kerb almost before she had arrived at the path that led up through the tangle of shrubbery to the house, and by the time she was at her front door at the top of the outdoor stairway his red tail-lights had disappeared around the corner at the far end of the street.

Karen let herself in, annoyed at herself for standing there and watching his departure like that. The cottage was chilly. It was going to be a cool night in spite of the earlier warmth of the day. She looked at her watch. Only ten; it hadn't been a long evening. She paced the floor restlessly, wondering if it was silly and hysterical of her to feel that something had gone badly wrong tonight. It *was* silly. There was nothing at all that she could put her finger on. . .except that Raif hadn't kissed her.

'Sorry about last night.' It was almost the first thing Raif said after she opened the door to him promptly at ten-thirty the next morning.

'Sorry for what?' she made herself say very casually. She hadn't slept well, battling against a stupid degree of disappointment, certain that he had decided to keep strictly to a casual friendship with her, and now he was apologising.

'I had things on my mind. . . I still have. Don't take any notice.'

'OK,' she said, imitating an American drawl and making him laugh.

Things on his mind. She wouldn't have guessed it this morning as they loaded her picnic contributions into the back of his car and drove to the triangular tongue of land that jutted between the mouth of the Columbia River and the ocean. He was a perfect tour guide, giving just the right amount of information about the two lighthouses which they walked to along neat tracks through green and overgrown vegetation.

'Want to sit and watch the sea for a while?' he asked when they had reached the clifftop lighthouse at North Head.

'Yes, please,' Karen said.

It was a savagely beautiful sweep of crashing ocean, rocky cliffs and soughing pines, and they found a sunny spot that was sheltered from the strong and rather chilly sea-breeze. From the pockets of his light beige windjacket, Raif pulled two small bottles of fruit juice and a packet of flaky cheese pastry biscuits.

'Hey, these weren't on our list of provisions!' Karen exclaimed.

'Something extra, in case we'd under-catered,' he said.

'Raiford, where did you live before you came here? Where were you born?' she asked suddenly, on impulse.

Last night, lying awake, she had realised that she had no idea, and that although they'd talked about many things together in odd moments by this time, his family and origins wasn't one of them.

'California,' he answered easily, setting at rest her momentary fear that there was some mystery to his past which he would be angry about having to reveal. 'Los Angeles, actually. . .and since that's a pretty big place, I'll be even more specific. We lived quite near Tinseltown itself—Hollywood—for most of my childhood years.'

'Glamorous!'

'Utterly the reverse.' His voice had hardened. 'My father hung around the movie scene, called himself a film producer. He adopted various elements of the lifestyle—the drinking, gambling, womanising—but I'm afraid he never produced a movie. Every now and then he'd make some money in a spectacular way, then lose it again almost as quickly.'

Karen nodded slowly, and he continued, telling the story of his mother's hard-working years and comparatively recent death, and his father's disappearance and lack of responsiveness to his only son.

'I could have stayed there and made money,' Raif went on. 'There was a stage when I considered cosmetic surgery as a specialty. It's a fascinating and necessary field. Damaged faces and bodies can be repaired miraculously after the most ghastly accidents or birth malformations these days. But in that city it's the face-lifts and tummy tucks that count, and I. . . Stupid to let it make me angry, but it does.'

He stopped speaking abruptly, picked up a pebble from the ground beside him and tossed it towards the cliff edge, where it skittered harmlessly on the rocks and grass, well short of its mark. Karen could tell that there were things he was leaving unsaid, but she didn't press him about it.

They sat for a while longer in silence. Raif broke it after several minutes to gesture towards the cliffs that stretched away from them southwards towards the mouth of the great Columbia River.

'Look at the washes of colour, paler and paler as the cliffs get further away. . .'

'Have you painted this——?' Karen began, then interrupted herself excitedly. 'That seascape in my surgery—the water-colour! That's from here, isn't it? And you painted it! How idiotic of me. I should have realised at once. You're very good, Raif!'

It wasn't the right thing to say, and she remembered too late that he had withdrawn and seemed angry that night in late June when she had asked about the brushstrokes of lemon-yellow and burnt orange on a sheet of water-colour paper in his kitchen. Goodness knew why he should be sensitive about the subject, but he was.

Now, for example, he only shrugged and muttered something that she didn't catch. She felt chastised by his manner, as if any fool would have known better than to talk about water-colours and landscapes to him. Then, just as she was beginning to wish that this had only been planned as a morning excursion, his arm came around her shoulder and he squeezed her, saying nothing, but with an apology in the gentle support of his touch.

She relaxed against his warmth. In an open-necked blouse of pale apricot and close-fitting cinnamon-brown cotton trousers, she was starting to feel a little cold. The sun was disappearing behind a woolly white cloud, and several more equally innocent ones made chasing shadows over the cliffs to the south.

As she stifled a shiver, his arm tightened around her, then he turned her into his embrace and they slid down into a grassy hollow and he kissed her—first her closed eyelids, then her cheeks, and finally her lips, as if still apologising for the private reaches of his mind where he would not yet allow her to go.

The sun emerged from the cloud again, coating them both with sleepy warmth as he caressed her with a mounting desire that was fully met by her own response. His chest was firm against her breasts and then he pulled away a little to coax the buttons of her collarless blouse undone so that he could nuzzle her teasingly with his lips above the low-cut cups of the lacy ivory silk bra she wore.

It was only when she heard a child's excited scream of laughter, and a mother's warning voice, 'Don't go too near the edge, Catherine!' that Karen remembered how public a place this actually was.

Several couples and family groups had passed behind them on the path while they were sitting in silence, and anyone could do what they had done and stray off the path to come closer to the cliffs for a better view.

Raif had already stiffened, and Karen half rolled on her side away from him, quickly putting fingers that trembled to the buttons of her blouse to fasten them again. It was an effort to curb the tide of arousal within her, and when she heard his careful breathing she knew that Raif was struggling against the same feelings.

'Look at the waves, Catherine!' The mother and her child came into view, and then the woman saw Karen and Raif. 'Oh, excuse me...'

'No need to apologise,' Raif said gruffly.

The woman smiled and turned away, chatting to her child. She had clearly guessed what she and Catherine had interrupted. The child stared at them for a moment longer, then giggled and whispered something to her mother. Karen flushed with embarrassment. The moment was thoroughly spoiled now.

Raif was on his feet and reaching a hand down to her. She took it and let him pull her up, reacting instantly again just to the deliberate caress of his thumb on her wrist. It was frightening how strongly she responded to him. While he was bending towards her as he pulled, his shirt came open a little across his chest. He wore nothing beneath, and Karen glimpsed the regular pattern of his dark hair. She was flooded with a longing to explore those hairs with her lips and cheeks, while her hands traced the long muscles of his thighs.

She felt weak with the effort of resisting these thoughts and the waves of feeling they produced deep in her body, and it was a relief when he spoke as he pulled her strongly by the hand back to the path. 'Come on. It's time we ate lunch.'

They returned to the car, took out their basket of cold but appetising foods and found a picnic table—a safe expanse of grey weathered wood which came between them as they ate, and dissipated the sizzling awareness that Karen still felt.

She had provided fruit and cheese, a tossed salad of lettuce, cucumber, tomato and avocado, apple juice and mineral water, while Raif had raided the best bakery and gourmet food store in the area, to come up with crusty wholemeal bread, unsalted butter, pâté, slices of exotically flavoured ham, and some beautifully made English pork pies, 'to make you feel at home'. Strawberry tartlets and a thermos of tea finished off the meal, which was sumptuous enough to distract Karen's attention from other more demanding and dangerous appetites.

The Lewis and Clark Interpretive Center was a further distraction, which both of them took advantage of. It was built almost on the site of the exploratory team's first view of the Pacific Ocean. The exhibits in the museum put together a fascinating picture of the epic journey, by the two explorers and their team from St Louis, Missouri, up the Mississippi and Missouri rivers, across the dividing range of the Rockies and down the tumultuous course of the Columbia to the sea.

It was far easier and safer to get caught up in the dramas and triumphs of a hundred and eighty-odd years ago than to question her feelings in the present, Karen found. They had lingered for longer over lunch and on their clifftop walk this morning than she had realised, and when they left the museum it was already after four.

As they began the drive homeward, they were still talking about the region and its history, and Karen hadn't thought about what she would do with the rest of the day. It was as they neared the turn-off to her own street in Ocean Park that Raif spoke after a small pause.

'Like to come to my place and see my paintings of this area? You can stay on for dinner and we'll cook up some pasta, if you're not doing anything else tonight.' His tone warned her not to probe him about his new openness on the subject of his painting.

'I'd like to very much,' Karen said. She'd invited Geoff and Rosalie Thorne across for a drink and a pot-luck meal tomorrow evening, but apart from household duties and some letters to friends in England that needed writing, she had nothing else planned for the weekend.

She relaxed back into the deep bucket-seat of his car. It was still the some old tank whose brakes had failed several weeks ago, but he had had them thoroughly overhauled, as well as checking every other important mechanical function. It would be nice to see his house again, and to see the historic village of Oysterville in the attractive late afternoon light of a sunny day.

Karen hadn't dared to explore the tiny town since that too-intense night at Raif's. With her increasingly complex feelings about him, she was too afraid that he would encounter her on one of the streets and conclude that she was prowling around his place like a lovesick adolescent—and that conclusion would at times have been uncomfortably close to the truth.

'Can I take a tour of the garden first?' she said when they arrived, and he took her round to the side of the house away from the street.

'These houses face a main street that no longer exists,' he told her. 'That's why what's now their back façade seems more imposing than the front. I suppose you know that? Oysterville was quite a town at one stage, but now there are only a couple of streets left, and the layout of the whole place has changed.'

'Why did you choose to live here?' They were wandering together across what had been the original front lawn, pausing at beds of flowers and looking back out towards Willapa Bay.

'I fell in love with the house,' he said simply.

'Was it like this?' She gestured at the neat paintwork and open stone-covered terrace as they approached the house again.

'No, very run down. I should have said I fell in love with what I thought I could do to it.'

'And you've certainly done it, Raif. It's worthy of a glossy spread in a lifestyle magazine.'

'No, it's too lived-in for that,' he answered, opening the door for her and revealing a pile of dirty washing in what must have once been the main entrance hall but was now a very adequate laundry and storeroom.

'True,' Karen laughed. 'And actually, I prefer the lived-in look. I feel sorry for any children in those showpiece homes.'

'Coffee, then paintings?'

'Yes, please.' Her reply was bright, but she had sensed a tension in his question. He wasn't looking forward to showing her his work at all, she could tell, and yet she'd made no secret of how she adored that seascape, even before she knew it was his.

She stood in the kitchen with him as he brewed coffee, studying the tall wooden dresser with its blue and white patterned plates, the tidy racks of herbs and spices, and the heavier shelves of jars and canisters, and she remembered the meal he had conjured up that stormy night in late June. Then he led the way up the polished wooden staircase to a large, sunny room that was clearly where he worked on his art.

Karen sipped her coffee as he brought out boards and canvases, sketch-pads and cardboard-mounted drawings. There were water-colours, charcoals, coloured crayons, and some oils, which seemed to be a new direction with which he was still experimenting.

Karen was careful with her comments, sensing the wariness and tension that stiffened his capable limbs into more rigid lines than usual, and the heavy frown that rarely left his high, tanned brow. His dark hair was untidy—as was hers, no doubt, after this morning's windy walk along the cliffs—and he made it worse by raking stiff fingers absently through it.

Her own hand tingled as she stifled a longing to smooth those wayward strands. Desperately, she searched for a comment to block out this dangerous resurgence of physical awareness, and, forgetting her earlier carefulness, blurted the first thing that came into her head.

'Have you sold many of them?'

'No,' he answered bluntly, 'I haven't. I haven't tried. I'm a doctor—that's important. This is purely a hobby.'

'Oh. Oh, all right,' Karen stammered, and there was an awkward silence, broken by his footsteps pacing with a resonant echo across the wooden floor as he put the unframed painting he was holding back in its position, stacked facing the wall with a line of its fellows.

'Anyway, you've seen enough,' he said. 'Come on.'

He shut the door of the room firmly behind them, although it had been open when they came upstairs, and it was as if he was shutting the door on that part of himself which was this intensely felt 'hobby', and shutting Karen out. Had she failed some kind of test in her reaction to his work?

But by the time they had re-entered the kitchen, and put their empty coffee-cups on the sink, his manner seemed cheerful again, as if he had deliberately thrown off that earlier emotion.

'Feel like making some pasta, then?'

'Making pasta?' Karen queried. 'I thought you meant making the sauce to go with it.'

'Well, we can limit ourselves to that, if you like. I do have the pre-fab stuff in plastic packets. But there's this rather handy machine too, and I think it's good fun.' He rested his hand on a shiny metal pasta-maker that was clamped to the end of the kitchen table. 'See. . . I have some dough already made. I'll put together a sauce and you can play pre-schooler and press it through this mould. You make flat sheets first, then this roller cuts it into ribbons—fettucine—or fine vermicelli.'

'It *does* look like fun,' Karen said, nodding.

Raif got out the dough, put on the radio, poured them each a glass of white wine, then started to make a sauce of tomato and garlic and olives and fresh herbs, while Karen passed her strips of dough back and forth through the rollers on an increasingly fine setting until they were ready to be cut into ribbons. It did feel a bit like kindergarten days, making messes with clay or play-dough, and she drank her wine a little too fast under the influence of the relaxed atmosphere, mellow music, and the appetising aroma of Raif's sauce. She didn't notice, either, when he refilled the glass, and so she drank that too.

He came over to check her work just as she'd hung the last of her long and slightly wobbly ribbons on a wooden stick suspended between two chairbacks.

'Whoops!' he said, rescuing one skinny strand. 'This one's about to break.'

'Yes, my sheets weren't very even at the edges, so some of the strips haven't quite worked,' Karen answered a little unsteadily.

'Water's boiling. We'll drop it in, shall we?'

He was about to gather up the strands, standing close to her so that she caught the scent of his aftershave, still faintly hovering around him even after the day spent largely outdoors. His face was only inches from her own, and suddenly the inevitable was happening again. His arms were softly around her and his lips were coaxing her own to part and respond, sending melting waves of awareness all through her.

She didn't stop to hold herself back. Why should she? They were two adults, equal, and free to give way to their passion and follow where it led with their whole hearts. . .weren't they?

'Raif,' she murmured longingly, starting to think of the ultimate consummation of her body's need, and knowing that she would soon be ready for it.

She felt the shoulder-straps of her bra slide off as his hands moved her clothing, and didn't care that two of the buttons on her blouse had come adrift on loose threads, exposing her rounded, pulsing breasts to his caressing touch.

'Karen, no. . . That's more than enough.'

Before she had time to take in the stiffening of his arm muscles, Raif had pushed himself away from her, leaving her vulnerable and chilled as cool air touched the tender skin of her nipples. Quickly she pulled at her bra and clutched the gaping sides of her blouse together with shaking hands.

'I'm sorry,' he was saying, staring at the floor and breathing heavily.

'Why? I don't understand. . .' she began, hearing the high note of pain in her own voice.

'This can't go on. I shouldn't have asked you here tonight. I might have known. . .'

'But why?' she repeated, not caring, yet, how desperate it sounded. There was a silence, then——

'For the commonest of reasons, I suppose,' he said, very slowly. 'Because I'm. . .' Again he hesitated for what seemed like a long time. Karen's heart was pounding. 'I'm involved with someone else.'

CHAPTER SEVEN

KAREN stumbled out of the white picket gate and started down the road towards Ocean Park, not caring that the gate had not latched behind her, and now banged back and forth on its hinges in the evening breeze. She wanted only to get home, home to the safety and solitude of her cottage. She had no car, it was several miles away, and she doubted that a taxi or bus would come cruising past, but it didn't matter. Her legs moved rapidly and rhythmically, and she was barely aware of them.

It had been quite early when they started cooking, and the low sun was still giving plenty of light. Summer traffic swished by at regular intervals. No one offered Karen a lift, and she would have refused if someone had. It simply looked as if she was out for some exercise in the late, pretty light.

She still burned with shame and misery at the memory of that revelatory scene. Every second of it.

'Is it Stephanie?' she had blurted as her first unthinking response.

'No, it isn't,' Raif had answered gently, and it was then that she had picked up her bag, turned, and fled, with the pasta water still boiling vigorously on the stove.

She had never suspected any involvement on his part! Oh, she had wondered about it at first, naturally. But she had noticed during her first visit to his lovely house that there was no sign of a female presence there. No woman had ever called to wait for him at the surgery, and as far as she knew no telephone messages ever awaited him at the end of the day in Stephanie's neat hand—'Jane will be late this evening.' 'Susan wants you to pick up some dry-cleaning for her on your way to the restaurant.' Nothing like that.

She felt an utter fool for having brought their receptionist into the picture with that blurted question. It sounded as if she had been casting about for an object for her jealousy, and his, 'No, is isn't,' had been honest, simple, and a little pitying.

Karen didn't want his pity! He should have told her long ago! The fact that she still didn't have the slightest clue who the woman could be wasn't important. He had been wrong to mislead her like that. . .

And yet they hadn't ever embarked on a real relationship, had they? That had existed largely in her own mind, a product of her own wishes and desires. It was her own foolishness she had to regret, rather than feeling any anger against Raiford Calvert. Perhaps this 'involvement' of his was a recent thing. Perhaps for a while he'd been torn between Karen and the unknown woman, and now he had made his decision. . .

She looked back along the road suddenly, terrified that he would have decided to follow her in order to offer a comfort and sympathy that was the last thing she wanted from him. No, no cars coming this way. But what was that, disappearing around the corner of the road, back towards Oysterville? Red brake-lights disguised the dark blue tail of a long, tank-like car. It was his, she was sure. He had been following her slowly at a distance, to make sure she seemed all right, guessing that she wouldn't want to be aware of his presence, and now that he was satisfied she was heading safely for home he had turned around again.

It seemed like the final humiliation. Would he sit down calmly and eat that fresh pasta with its deliciously savoury sauce? Karen's appetite, recently quite sharp, had completely gone and she knew she would eat nothing tonight.

She thought of how calm and almost complacent she had been at times over the past few weeks about the idea of an involvement with Raif. How could she have descended to that level of self-delusion? Complacent, when she now knew how badly she wanted him, and how much she loved him. She had thought of love growing gradually and safely between them, and it was only now, when the possibility of that love had been so brutally stripped away by his words, that she realised how deeply he had grown into her soul.

Again and again the thought drummed in her mind. What a fool she was!

It was quite dark by the time she got home, and she should have been exhausted after the long walk at the fast pace she had maintained the whole way. When the sun had disappeared it had became colder, and her ears were aching now and her arms covered in goose-bumps. Numbly, she ran herself a hot, deep bath and lay in it till the water cooled to tepid, the same thoughts continuing to drum round and round, like billiard balls hitting one another on a green felt table. What an utter fool she was to have let herself get so involved and to have betrayed herself so openly to him! How could she salvage her self-respect and her peace of mind? How could she douse the painful flame of this love?

Somehow, she got through the night, and through the day that followed. Rising early and cleaning the cottage thoroughly, then slinging a towel over her shoulder and tramping across the beach in her sea-green figure-hugging costume for a swim in the cold Pacific surf reminded her that there were pleasures in her life here that would remain regardless of Raif. The buffeting waves gave her an appetite too, after last night's emotional fasting, and she returned to the cottage to make a full plate of eggs and bacon, sausages and tomato, and crisp toasted rolls with coffee.

It wasn't a breakfast she usually enjoyed. Cholesterol! Saturated fats! her medical mind exclaimed in horror. But today it was just right, and it restored her enough to see her through the day.

It was good to have Rosalie and Geoff over too, chatting with them for quite a while over drinks and appetisers, then enjoying a simple meal of salad and a hearty soup. Life goes on, Karen thought to herself with bitter humour, regardless of these trivial heartbreaks and humiliations. Geoff and Rosalie hadn't even noticed that anything was wrong.

Neither did Stephanie Zeigler the next morning at the surgery when Karen entered, even though she disappeared into her own room more quickly than usual. . . Yes, over the past couple of weeks, she had got into the unfortunate habit of lingering in the waiting-room chatting to Stephanie until Raif appeared, so that she could see him and smile at him before the start of her working day. No more of that now. At least they finished early on Mondays, and had a break before evening surgery hours.

An elderly lady, Mrs Hart, was Karen's first patient, sitting down very cautiously in the stiff-backed chair as if she didn't trust her own balance.

'It's just the same old problem come back again,' she said. 'My dizziness. I've run out of the prescription Dr Thomas gave me.'

Karen did some routine tests and looked back through Mrs Hart's file. The cause of the dizziness had never clearly been identified, even after consultation with a specialist in Portland. It seemed almost certain that there was some problem in the finely tuned inner ear, but this area was so delicate that any surgical probing would almost certainly result in deafness. Mrs Hart's dizziness might disappear for six months at a time, and then recur when she was least expecting it.

Karen prescribed an antibiotic to combat possible inflammation in the inner ear, and gave Mrs Hart a pamphlet about reducing blood-pressure, although the level was not seriously above normal range. Meanwhile, Mrs Hart was happy to chat.

'It's lovely to have you and Dr Calvert in a shared practice like this. The waiting-room is looking so nice, and if I couldn't see you one day, I'd be just as happy to see him. I do wish you both all the best with it.'

Karen smiled and thanked her patient, then Mrs Hart added confidingly, 'But I do wish Dr Calvert would get married. People want him to stay in the area, but a single man so often moves on.'

Dr Madigan could only nod and murmur a conventional response. It wasn't her place to give away the secret of Dr Calvert's involvement with a local woman, and anyway, she didn't know if marriage plans were in the wind yet. In fact, she knew almost nothing about the situation at all. 'I'm involved with someone else.' Perhaps it *wasn't* a local woman. Somehow it hurt all the more because she was so much in the dark about his private life.

Mrs Hart made her hesitant way out of the surgery, and the next patient, a young mother with a tetchy, feverish six-month-old girl, came in straight away. There was little Karen could really do, other than make some checks to eliminate any potentially serious causes. It looked like a very mild twenty-four-hour virus, and the baby's temperature was not seriously elevated. She was clearly well cared for and in good general health. Noting down her weight, Karen saw that little Amy had gained a very satisfactory three pounds since her last visit.

Next came a local commercial fisherman, Dave Barton, who was usually Dr Calvert's patient.

'It's such a minor thing, I said to Miss Zeigler I didn't care if she did it herself. She suggested I might like to take a look at the new doctor...and I'm glad I did.' He gave a wicked wink, and Karen laughed.

'I'm sure the novelty of my existence will wear off soon,' she said.

'But the novelty of your charming appearance won't, he capped, with mischievous gallantry, then became suddenly practical. 'Why I'm here is that my ears need a good syringe, that's all. Does everyone need it from time to time? My wife says she's never had it done in her life.'

'Everyone's different,' Karen said, as she took out an instrument with which to examine the ear. 'Some people just seem to get a build-up that can temporarily affect their hearing...'

'That's right,' he said energetically. 'I feel as if I'm listening to the world through a thick feather pillow.'

His ears were soon clear again after their scouring with a fine jet of water, and he was grinning with pleasure at the difference it made. A sparrow chattered and chirruped outside the window at that moment. 'Is that a bird?' he said. 'It sounds like an orchestra!'

Outside in the waiting-room, Karen heard him exchange a quick joke with Raif, and she had to resist the temptation to wander out herself to ask Stephanie for a coffee. Perhaps once she'd said hello to her medical partner in a casual, friendly way, she wouldn't feel this pain about the night before last.

At that moment, however—perhaps fortunately—Stephanie opened the door and brought in a steaming mug.

'Mrs Dennis isn't here yet—she's *always* late—so I thought you might like this.'

'Mmm, lovely,' Karen said, trying to ignore the deep tone of Raif's laugh in the background.

'Shall I just send her straight in when she arrives?'

'Yes, I'll flip through her notes now,' Karen said, stifling a brief sigh.

In short it was a routine day, the usual mixture of common complaints, chronic problems in some elderly patients, false alarms, and always the need to watch out for the serious warning symptoms that could catch a careless GP unawares. This was why a general practitioner needed imagination, human understanding, and a wider knowledge than many people realised. A patient might never get to that heart or kidney specialist if their GP hadn't picked up the warning signals first, from among an apparently routine set of complaints.

Karen was musing a little too determinedly about this aspect of general practice when her last patient of the day session entered at just after two. He was a thin and rather unhealthy looking man of about thirty, whom she had not encountered before, and he sat down with a mixture of edginess and brash confidence that would have put Karen immediately on the alert if she hadn't been wishing it was a quarter to three.

She could hear Raif's voice in the waiting-room talking to Stephanie and she didn't *want* those deep, resonant tones to have any power over her, but unfortunately they did. What a pity she couldn't just get up and go home, where she wouldn't be forced to think about him. . .

'I think I'm stressed out and depressed,' the man was saying. What was his name again? Karen glanced tiredly down at his file. Steve Billings. 'I seem to be having these mood swings, and I get headaches too.'

Karen nodded and listened, and asked a couple of standard questions. Depression and stress. All right. There were a number of different kinds of medication that would help control those problems. She named one that was relatively benign and free from side-effects, wondering if she should suggest some counselling as well as just the superficial solution of medication. . .

Her patient shifted restlessly, scratching at the rather

dirty knee of his jeans and sniffing loudly. 'Couldn't you give me something else?'

He quickly and fluently reeled off the names of three prescription drugs he had had 'a couple of years ago', and suddenly something clicked in Karen's mind. For a moment she didn't know how to respond. What was best? Pretend she hadn't cottoned on to him, and send him away with a placebo prescription, or confront him openly?

Before she had made up her mind, the door opened— no knock first—and Raif stood there.

'Could I see you, please, Dr Madigan?' he asked.

'We're almost finished, Doc,' Steve Billings said, his tone rising with anxiety as he sensed the threat to his goal.

'In here, Dr Calvert?' Karen put in, a little unsteadily, her cheeks growing hot at the very sight of him.

'Yes, please. Wait outside, would you, Mr Billings?'

'Sure. . .' The cheerfulness was forced.

Raif stood holding the door till the thin, gangly form had passed through, moving with an appearance of jauntiness that no longer fooled Karen at all. She felt sick, though, at how close she had come to being taken in. The door shut with a deliberate click and Raif came quickly towards her, not sitting in front of her desk but passing it so that she had to stand to face him directly. For the first time, she hated the new short haircut, which she'd had freshly trimmed a week ago, and longed for her long-gone waist-length tresses, that could at times like this hang like a concealing curtain around her face.

'You were about to write out those prescriptions for him like an obedient schoolgirl, weren't you?' he rasped in a low tone. Both of them were aware that Steve Billings was only just outside the door.

'I——'

'Pull yourself together, Karen!' He gripped her

shoulders with hard hands and shook her once, then released her abruptly. 'I know this is hard——'

'I'm fine. Please can we——?'

He didn't let her finish, but ploughed on angrily. 'You wrote out the wrong prescription for old Mrs Tanguy today. A completely unrelated drug. It's lucky she'd just come for a repeat and knew what she should have been getting.'

'Oh. . . I. . . That's terrible!' Karen sank into her chair, cheeks burning and knees weak.

'Yes, it is,' he answered forcefully. 'I'm not going to say, "Don't feel bad about it," because I want you to feel bad.'

'I *wasn't* going to give Steve Billings the drugs he wanted. . . Don't say anything, Raif,' Karen added quickly, seeing his anger rise as he thought she was making excuses. 'I'd realised by the end that he was an addict. But you're right—it was something I should have seen straight away. Mrs Tanguy. . . I have no excuse. Don't worry, though. It won't happen again.'

'It had better not, Karen. We're in a partnership, remember. Any mistake you make affects my reputation, and I'm not having that. You own this building and I'm paying you rent. In a sense that gives you power, but I've been in this area longer than you, and if I leave to set up my own practice again, it'll be you that loses out. Don't forget that.'

'All right, Raif. You've made your point,' Karen said, her own anger rising now. She had accepted full blame, and had seen the consequences of today's mistake for herself. There was no need for him to go on about it.

'No, I haven't,' he said crisply. 'There's more. Stephanie managed to cover for you. She told Mrs Tanguy that you'd decided to try a different drug company's version of the same medication, but that I'd write out a prescription for the one she was used to, if she was happier with that—and I did. Mrs Tanguy is vague and good-natured, and it won't occur to her to talk to anyone about this, but if it had been Dulcie Barnett, the story—heavily embroidered and very dangerous for you—would be all over Long Beach Peninsula by now.'

'All *right*, Raiford!' She leapt to her feet with flaming cheeks and a hard sparkle in her green eyes. 'For heaven's sake, can we leave it at that?'

'I had to say it, Karen. . .'

But she hadn't stayed to listen to these gentler words. He saw her pick up the black bag that contrasted with her green linen dress, the surgery door slammed behind her, and then he heard her fling an excuse to Stephanie as she crossed the waiting-room with small quick steps— 'I have an appointment at the bank and I'm late.'

He left her surgery slowly, shutting the door and then turning to Stephanie. 'Where's Steve Billings?'

'He left straight away,' Stephanie said casually. She must have heard the two doctors in Karen's surgery, but she gave no sign that she knew something was amiss, bless her. 'He knew he wasn't going to get those drugs, so he didn't stick around. I wonder who he'll try to con next.'

'He might leave town again,' Raif said. 'He probably only came to sponge some money off his brother, heard there was a new doctor in the area and thought he'd try his luck.'

He wasn't really thinking about what he was saying, but conversation was always a safe way to mask awkward emotions.

'Can you lock up, Steffie?' he said now. 'And I'll unlock for surgery tonight.'

'Of course. See you later, then.'

He clattered down the steps, not bothering with the light jacket that hung on a hook behind his surgery door.

He wouldn't need it before coming back here this evening. That scene with Karen had raised his temperature too. Awful, it had been, and he had hated having to do it. She was right, he had gone on too harshly and too long, but it had seemed best—to get her anger up as well as his own. Anger provided a safety, sometimes, from things you didn't want to feel.

He walked on the beach for a long time that afternoon, thinking, and was almost too late back to the surgery to open it up for evening hours as he had promised to do. Both Karen and Stephanie arrived hard on his heels, and mercifully the first patient less than a minute after that.

Karen waited until she heard Raif's 'Goodnight' to Stephanie before she emerged from her surgery at a quarter past nine. After today's lapse, she had been over-meticulous with each case and had finished some time after Raif's last patient had departed.

'I'll lock up,' she said to Stephanie, and the young blonde receptionist nodded cheerfully.

When Karen was alone in the waiting-room, she went to the appointment book, and ran her finger down tomorrow's page. Yes, Harry Greenidge was coming in, and she hadn't yet made the thorough study of his file that she wanted to do. There seemed no reason not to stay and do that work now—it would be a very welcome distraction from the day's tumult of feeling—so she got the file out of the cabinet, found a bulky and very specialised book on certain types of cancer and sat down in one of the low, comfortable waiting-room chairs to read.

It was nearly an hour later when she was startled by a long peal of the telephone. The answer machine clicked and switched itself into action after three rings, and Karen was tempted to let it deliver its bland, recorded announcement. It was pure coincidence that she was here this late at night, and the alternative telephone numbers were quite clearly given in the message that Stephanie had recorded, as well as a suggestion that any urgent problem be taken to the hospital emergency department.

Somehow, though, it went against the grain just to sit here listening to it, and before the message ended Karen had picked up the telephone receiver and spoken a breathless, 'Hello?'

'Oh. . . What?' came a distorted male voice.

'This is Dr Madigan speaking. I've disconnected the machine,' Karen said crisply. 'Can I help you?'

'Doctor? It's Harry Greenidge. I'm feeling real bad—I mean *real* bad! I've never felt this bad before!'

Harry! Fresh from her reading about his case, Karen felt her heart thud with foreboding. 'What's happening, Harry?'

'My wife wants me to get to the hospital. She's getting the car out of the garage. I thought I'd ask Dr Calvert——'

'Your wife's right, Harry,' Karen interrupted quickly. 'Don't tire yourself with talk. I'll drive to the hospital now and start the procedure of getting you admitted. They'll be expecting you by the time you get there.'

'But Dr Calvert might——'

'Don't worry about bringing Dr Calvert into it. He isn't here, and I don't know how to reach him.' This wasn't quite the truth. It was more than likely Raif would be at home. . .Unless, she thought with a sudden stab of pain, he was spending the night with the mysterious woman whose 'involvement' with him had shattered Karen's own naïve hopes only two days ago.

But it wasn't their awkwardness today and over the weekend that made Karen reluctant to involve her professional partner. It was Raif's preconception about Harry Greenidge. She was convinced that something was seriously wrong, and that a biopsy was necessary tonight. She didn't want to have to convince Raif, or face any suggestion that she was just looking for a way to prove herself after today's mistake.

Quickly she checked and locked the surgery, and hurried to her car, wanting a chance to talk to the surgeon alone before Harry Greenidge and his wife arrived. If she was right in what she suspected, it could be a question of life and death. . .

'You didn't have to wait.' The surgeon, Andrew Gladwin, came towards her, tall, bearded and loose-limbed.

'I wanted to know.' Karen stood up tiredly and blinked in the glaring fluorescent lights of the hospital waiting-room where she had been sitting vainly trying to distract herself with magazines.

It was in the early hours of the morning now, and it would be hard to keep alert tomorrow, but she couldn't leave without knowing what had happened, when she had laid herself on the line tonight, arguing for that biopsy.

'Did you find anything?' she asked, masking the anxiety she felt.

'*Find* anything? He would have been dead by morning if we hadn't operated tonight,' Andrew Gladwin said.

'And now?'

'I can't say for certain, of course, but there's a very strong chance that he'll be one hundred per cent for a good many years to come.'

Karen felt weak with relief. She had been right. What was more important, she had answered that phone, hadn't belittled Harry's cry for help and had acted in time, so that his life was saved. It made her shiver to think how easy it would have been for events to go the other way.

'The intestine had completely blocked, and his whole system was poisoning itself,' the surgeon was saying.

'Why didn't the colonoscopy pick it up? The growth must have been there three months ago,' Karen said.

'He seems to have an unusually long colon,' Mr Gladwin explained, shrugging his shoulders to loosen the tension that had built up in his limbs during the delicate and difficult operation. 'The equipment simply didn't reach that far, I guess.'

'He'd manufactured so many complaints over the years that Dr Calvert was convinced it was just another case of crying wolf,' Karen said. 'Understandable in the circumstances,' she added quickly, defending her partner, in spite of everything she felt about him in her heart now.

'What made you think differently?' the surgeon asked.

'Brute stubbornness?' She laughed. 'No, I suppose I was approaching the case with a fresh eye. To me, he looked unwell, as he said he was. I was reading up on it tonight late at the surgery when he rang—and thank goodness he did, and that I answered, or he mightn't have got to you in time!'

'You'd better get off home, Dr Madigan,' the surgeon said. 'You're starting to sound a little strung out.'

'Oh, am I?' Karen forced a laugh. 'Yes, it's been a long day.'

'But it's ended well.'

'Yes, it has.' There was little left to say, and Karen saw the middle-aged surgeon rubbing his eyes. 'Goodnight, then,' she said, and left the hospital.

It was hard to know how to bring up the subject of Harry Greenidge's case with Raif the next morning. She had to tell him, of course, but her upright inner being winced at the idea of getting any personal mileage out of it. In the end, she waited until their much-needed lunch break arrived, and when Stephanie had left the building to get sandwiches for each of them from a take-away bar down the road, Karen knocked on Raiford's surgery door.

'Come in!'

She did so. He was still at his desk, white shirt sleeves rolled to the elbows, finishing off some work on this morning's files. He looked up with a neutrally friendly expression in his grey eyes. 'What's up?'

Karen took a deep breath and plunged into the story, wasting no words. 'Harry Greenidge was operated on last night for cancer of the colon. Andrew Gladwin removed the growth and a section of the colon. There was a complete blockage.'

'How was he admitted? Had he collapsed?'

'No, I admitted him. I'd stayed back here for a while last night and he rang, quite distressed. The idea that he was malingering just didn't seem tenable any more, so I had them schedule an emergency biopsy. Perhaps I should have talked it over with you first. . .' She trailed off.

'No,' Raiford answered slowly. 'You were the last doctor to see him. . .' He paused. 'I'm rather bowled over by this. It's a case of my getting over-confident in my perceptions about human behaviour.'

'No,' Karen put in quickly, seeing his real distress. 'You're being too harsh on yourself. The colonoscopy showed a clear result, and so did the other tests.'

'It doesn't make sense,' Raif said, and Karen told him about Andrew Gladwin's discovery that the colon was unusually long. She was daring to breathe normally again now, after feeling a nebulous fear about what his response would be. *Would* he think she was gloating over her own success, showing it off to him to counteract yesterday's mistakes? It did not seem that way.

'Well, Karen, you should feel very pleased with yourself, and I hope you do,' he said.

'I'm pleased that he's going to be all right,' Karen

prevaricated. 'I rang the hospital this morning, and——'

'Granted,' Raif interrupted. 'I'm pleased too. I like Harry, in spite of the cynicism you detected in my earlier medical notes. But, leaving that aside, don't feel that you can't enjoy the professional triumph as well. It'll be good for the partnership. Good for us. I'll go and see Harry soon, and talk to Andrew Gladwin as well. You were a little frightened about telling me, weren't you?'

'Yes, I was,' Karen admitted. Why was he always so open and blunt? She'd lost count of the number of confessions—small and large—that he'd forced from her in this way.

'No, as I said, it's good for us that this has happened. . .but I must get these notes finished.'

It was a clear dismissal, and Karen left the attractively set up room, closing the door behind her.

What had he meant by the last, twice-repeated statement? she wondered. 'Good for us,' he had said. In what sense was he using the word 'us'? Professionally? No, it sounded as if it was a subtle reference to Saturday's revelation. He was too perceptive. He hadn't referred to her emotional flight from his house and her long pent-up walk home, but he had known how upset she was, and he had known it was important for them to find a way of restoring emotional equilibrium.

And her anger yesterday. . . Had he deliberately opened up that vent for her feelings? Now, today, with her status as a medical practitioner confirmed by the successful result of Harry Greenidge's operation, Raif thought she'd be 'on the mend' emotionally as well. He was probably relieved. Any threat to their professional partnership had been neutralised, and, from the very beginning of their acquaintance, it seemed that it was his work that he cared most about. Yes, to the extent of making love to her until he'd got what he wanted. . .

The nagging voice of reason told her that this didn't quite fit the facts, that he hadn't faked his physical response to her during those burning kisses they had shared, but it scarcely helped her now to mull over the whys and wherefores of the past. There had been times when she had trusted him absolutely, and other times when the force of her dislike had been equally strong. There was no clear-cut right or wrong.

They had a working relationship that could be very good in time, the personal part of his life was now taken up with another woman, and that was all there was to it.

CHAPTER EIGHT

'IT's nearly two weeks since Jenny Delancey had her pap smear,' Stephanie said to Karen on a Wednesday eight days later, 'and she hasn't called to hear the result. It showed an abnormality. . .'

She held out the pathology report and Karen took it, frowning. Nothing major, but it needed follow-up and careful explanation.

'I'd better call her myself,' she said. 'I'll do it now.' It was the end of the day's surgery, a quiet one, and therefore not yet five o'clock. 'Can I have her file?'

Stephanie went to the filing cabinet, crabbed her fingers quickly through it, pulled out a slim file and gave it to Karen. Raif emerged from his surgery just then.

'There was a long-distance call for you, Raif,' Stephanie said. 'From Los Angeles—Arlene.'

'Arlene?' Raif echoed the name in a tone that Karen had never heard from him before, and she felt a fiery dart stab inside her. He'd said it the way a man said a name that was very important, the name of a woman who was important in his life.

Quickly, she went into her surgery, sat at her desk and opened Jenny Delancey's file. She looked at her watch. Still only five to five. Well, it was less than a minute since she had last looked. Mrs Delancey was probably still at work. She had regular nine-to-five hours at a local bank, so it would be timely to call her there.

Firmly and deliberately, Karen put the name Arlene out of her mind. She had no proof that this was Raif's mysterious involvement, but she was sure of it none the less. It hurt, but there was nothing she could do about that. Jenny Delancey was more important. A doctor had to be careful when giving this sort of news, and Karen knew it was vital to take the necessary time to answer all Jenny Delancey's questions—preferably before she even asked them.

Was it fair to phone her at work, or would it be best to wait until later in the evening when she would be home and could absorb the news in complete privacy?

'I'll try now,' Karen decided. 'It shouldn't be put off.' She dialled the bank's number, getting put through to Mrs Delancey with no trouble, and ascertaining that she was alone and free of pressing work at that moment.

'I'm ringing about the result of your pap smear, Mrs Delancey,' she said.

'Oh, how stupid of me! I completely forgot to call and check as you asked me to. I'm so sorry. Now you've had to chase me up. Is it normal?' Jenny said.

'Well, no, it's not,' Karen answered.

She heard the young married woman's surprised and startled, 'Oh!' Women of twenty-seven didn't expect to hear this.

Quickly and carefully, Karen explained that the abnormality was only the very earliest of warning signals, and simply showed that some cells were present which could, if left unobserved and untreated, develop into cervical cancer in a few years' time. The next step was an examination by a gynaecologist, who might then decide that some simple laser surgery was called for. Following that, pap smears would take place a little more often for the next couple of years, and, if no further abnormal results showed up, the regular annual smear test would be quite adequate.

Once she had been reassured about all this, Jenny Delancey was calm and seemed quite happy about booking an appointment with the gynaecologist, to whom Karen would write a referral letter. When she put down the phone, Karen was glad she had made the effort to pull herself out of over-emotional thoughts about Raif. A less careful and concerned explanation to Jenny Delancey might have resulted in a fear and panic that was quite unnecessary.

In the waiting-room, she found Stephanie starting to lock up. Raif had already gone, taking the day's tests to the pathology lab, but probably wanting to get home quickly so he could return that long-distance call.

Karen herself didn't go straight home, needing to stop at the supermarket to stock up on household provisions. She hadn't made a list, and was walking slowly up and down each aisle, picking things off the shelves as they caught her eye, with a metal shopping trolley squeaking erratically in front of her, when she saw a familiar figure coming towards her, also wheeling a trolley.

It was Barbara Stenlow. She smiled stiffly at Karen, then stopped her trolley in the centre of the aisle. 'Hello, Dr Madigan.'

'Hello, Barbara. How are you?' Karen answered coolly. After what Raif had told her about the woman's underhand bad-mouthing, it was difficult to make her greeting a friendly one.

'I'm very well, thank you,' the older woman replied. She wore a soft slate-blue dress that suited her well and made her look quite attractive.

Karen wondered about all those years Barbara had spent working for Dr Thomas. Was Raif right? Had she cherished an unreturned passion for the older doctor all through that time? If so, it seemed like a waste.

'I'm very much enjoying working for Dr Rebbeck,' Barbara was saying, a self-conscious glow appearing on her cheeks.

'I'm glad to hear it.' Karen smiled carefully. 'Our new partnership is working out well too.'

'Oh, good,' said Miss Stenlow.

'Goodbye, then,' Karen finished with a last smile, then pushed her trolley onwards in the opposite direction.

It had been an easy enough exchange, with outward politeness on both sides. With a new working life now, and possibly a newly growing set of feelings for Dr Rebbeck, Barbara surely had nothing left to gain by remaining hostile towards Karen. Dr Thomas's wishes had almost been fulfilled now. Dr Calvert was working in the practice, even if it was not legally his.

You couldn't call a romantic feeling that survived unrequited for fifteen years 'love', Karen thought. Well, it was love of a kind, but not a healthy kind when carried to the lengths Barbara had gone to. It became obsession, a fantasy, insidiously destructive and dangerous. It drowned out and stifled the healthy elements of the original feeling—respect, care, friendship—and replaced them with hero-worship, possessiveness, and martyrdom.

Could the same thing ever happen to me? Karen wondered with a sudden shudder. Could this awful longing for Raif ever turn into what Barbara had felt? Surely not! And yet she ought not to dismiss the idea just like that. With a sinking heart, she knew that now— today!—was the time to take action to stamp out what she felt about Raiford Calvert.

Strangely, fate came to her assistance that very night. She was in the kitchen unpacking the shopping bags when there was a knock at the front door and Rosalie Thorne stood there, her wavy grey hair a little wild as usual.

'You haven't started cooking?' she said anxiously.

'No, I haven't,' Karen answered.

'Because I'm hoping you'll come across for a meal tonight. Please do,' she added quickly, seeing Karen's hesitation.

It would be lovely to go, but they were so generous

with their hospitality, she was sometimes afraid that she was building up a hopeless debt to them. But Rosalie was still speaking. 'My son's visiting us unexpectedly for a week or two from San Francisco. I'm terrified that, if I don't provide some excitement for him, he won't make it "or two" and will be gone again by the weekend. Do you mind being my bait?'

'Not at all,' Karen laughed, 'if you think I'll be any use. . .'

'He's very nice, Karen,' Rosalie said, suddenly more serious. 'But he'd been living with a girl for seven years and she's just walked out on him. Another man, I gather. Glenn's not the type to do anything silly, and he's hiding it well, but it's hit him hard.'

'Oh, dear!' Karen said. 'Seven years!' It put her own new pain into a better perspective, as had the encounter with Barbara at the supermarket.

'Yes. Of course we were always hoping they'd marry. We were. . . Well, I couldn't say we adored her, but we got to be fond of her. And I'm afraid child-rearing manuals don't cover what to say to your thirty-year-old in this situation.' Rosalie laughed helplessly. 'It was much easier worrying about toilet-training.'

'Of course I'll come, then,' Karen said. 'Just let me put the shopping away and change into something fresh, and I'll be right over. Is there anything I can bring? I've got a bottle of wine in a cupboard here somewhere.'

In fact, she'd bought it last week in preparation for one of the Thornes' impromptu invitations, which had brought her into contact with some interesting people over the summer.

'Lovely, then,' Rosalie said. 'We'll see you soon.'

Glenn Thorne rose politely to shake Karen's hand when she entered the room wearing a silky mauve dress that flattered the slim shape and proportioned curves of her tall figure, and contrasted with her green eyes, making them glow against the purple tones of the light eye make-up she wore.

'Pleased to meet you.' He was tall, with a heavy thatch of dark reddish hair and beard, and stooped down a little—perhaps as a physical response to the hurt of his newly ended relationship. Karen smiled brightly at him and murmured a friendly greeting, but she could see then, and as the evening progressed, that he was only going through the motions.

Rosalie and Geoff masked their anxiety, but watched carefully to make sure he ate, and encouraged any sign of cheerfulness that they saw in him.

'Have you been inland yet to the mountains?' he asked Karen towards the end of the meal.

'No, I've really not strayed off the peninsula since I came here,' she had to confess.

'You must see Mount St Helens,' Glenn said. 'That is, if you're at all interested in nature and its forces.'

'Oh, I am,' Karen answered. 'I've intended to go, but. . .well, setting up the practice here has taken a lot of time and energy. I've spent most of the summer on the beach.'

'Why don't you take her, Glenn?' Rosalie put in eagerly, seeing the opportunity of a healthily distracting outing for her son, in youthful company.

Karen felt a little embarrassed. Poor Glenn was on the spot now! She stepped in carefully. 'I'm sure you have friends to see. . .'

'No, let's do it,' he answered suddenly. 'I think you'd enjoy it.'

'And you'll get restless here, Glenn,' his father said.

'So. . . Are you free at the weekend?' Glenn asked.

'Yes,' Karen replied.

Too free. Two weeks ago, she might have assumed she'd be spending at least part of the time with Raif. Instead, she'd been half-heartedly thinking today that she might contact Suzanne Price, the hairdresser who had been her first acquaintance in Long Beach. They'd seen each other a couple of times over the summer and got on reasonably well, although they'd never be one another's closest friend. A trip to Mount St Helens would occupy a whole day.

'Sunday?' Glenn was asking.

'Yes, all right. I'll look forward to it,' she agreed sincerely, and when he suggested a movie on Friday night she agreed to that as well.

Karen was the first to arrive at the surgery the next morning, having volunteered to be the one to open up, since Stephanie had an early morning errand to run. As she passed the building in her car, slowing to manoeuvre into a nearby parking place, she saw that someone was already waiting, standing restlessly on the steps, then taking a few paces down the street and back again. This happened sometimes, but it was usually a man on his way to work hoping to be squeezed in, or an anxious mother with a sick child.

This, on the other hand, was a very expensively dressed and glamorous woman of about Karen's own age. . . No, perhaps a few years older. The details began to fill in as Karen got out of her car and approached the surgery. The woman wore expensive black leather shoes, with spiky heels and an unusual cut that made Karen think, Italian leather, and a matching black suit with short skirt, square-shouldered jacket and a cream blouse beneath that was open-necked. . .not to say low-cut. It looked like an outfit designed for the advertising empires of New York, not for the backwaters of Washington, and contrasted strongly with Karen's own full-skirted short-sleeved dress in an abstract, pastel-toned pattern.

'Are you waiting for surgery hours?' Karen asked as she reached the blonde woman.

'Oh. . . I. . .'

'I mean, do you have an appointment, or did you just want to see if we could fit you in?' Karen elaborated.

For a moment the woman hesitated, studying Karen with narrowed eyes, then, 'If you could fit me in. . .'

'I'll see what we can do. Come in, would you? I'll check the book.'

Karen unlocked the door, ushered the woman in and quickly opened blinds and windows to let in fresh balmy air. She had picked up the appointment book and was about to say, 'Please sit down,' when the stranger spoke. She had been studying the prints on the wall, and, as she turned away, the mane of artfully careless curls bounced a little stiffly, as if held in place by a little too much styling mousse.

'Is this painting an original?' she asked.

'Yes, it is, as a matter of fact,' Karen answered carefully. It was one of Raif's, but this was the first patient who had ever asked about it.

'I can't see a signature,' the woman went on.

'No, there isn't one,' Karen lied.

Actually, there *was* one, but it was nearly hidden by the frame. The upper curves of an 'R' and a 'C' were all that was visible, and they simply looked liked brush strokes in the impressionistic landscape. Raif had never told her to protect his anonymity like this, and she wasn't quite sure why she had done it. Nevertheless, she added a more definite, 'Just an anonymous hobby-artist's, I imagine. It dates from Dr Thomas's time.'

'An anonymous hobby-artist,' the woman echoed, giving the words an emphasis and touching the wide frame with one very long and very red acrylic nail.

Karen found herself addressing the woman in her mind. You shouldn't dress up like that, girl! It doesn't suit you! The face, dwarfed by its halo of curls, wasn't a truly beautiful one, but it had some strength of bone-structure in spite of a strangely characterless nose. In Karen's opinion—humble and amateur, of course—a more natural, casual look would have suited the stranger much better. Heavy foundation, bright lipstick artfully extending the lip-line and dramatic eye-shadow added up to too much make-up, as well. Still, it was purely a matter of personal taste.

'Now, you'd like to see a doctor this morning if possible,' Karen said briskly, crackling the pages of the appointment book as she flicked through it until she reached today's page.

Feet cantered on the wooden steps outside at that moment, and Karen recognised Raif's energetic early morning tread. When he arrived at the surgery each day, he always looked as if he'd been up for several healthy hours already, working with carefully gloved hands—a doctor couldn't work with earth-stained fingers—in his garden.

The door to the waiting-room swung open and he entered, then stopped abruptly. 'Arlene!'

The black-suited woman flicked a slightly embarrassed glance at Karen, then said, 'Hello, Raif. Don't say anything. It was an impulse. I took a week off and hopped on a flight last night. Then it got delayed and came in too late for me to call you, so I stayed in Portland overnight and rented a car first thing this morning.'

'A week,' Raif said.

'Yes. And I'm afraid I've let your secretary think I wanted an appointment.' Again the guilty glance at Karen.

'Not secretary. Partner,' he said tersely, giving an irritated glance at his fellow doctor. 'Stephanie stayed with the new partnership. I'm sure I told you.'

'I'd better. . .' Karen didn't bother to finish the sentence. It was purely an exit line, accompanied by a vague 'busy' gesture as she went towards her surgery door. Raif's look had told her clearly that the two of them wanted to be alone.

'An impulse, you say,' Raif said, taking Arlene's hand and not bothering to lower his voice.

'Yes.'

'And these nails? A surgeon can't perform with talons like that.'

'You're right. Another impulse. When the flight was delayed I went to the beautician at LA airport to fill in time.'

Karen closed her door and the voices were reduced to sketchy sounds, rising and falling but not identifiable as words. She sat down behind her desk and pressed cool fingers to her hot cheeks. This was Arlene. The other 'involvement' in Raif's life? She must be.

A long-distance relationship. It happened these days. Very modern. Conflicting careers that were both important. A decision to delay the channelling of choices that inevitably happened with marriage. Raif's comment about those red nails had made it clear that Arlene was a surgeon. Two doctors could well afford shuttling back and forth on planes every few weeks to see one another. Perhaps that was the real reason why Raif contented himself with such an old car. He had kept quiet about such trips, but then Karen and Stephanie rarely talked about how they spent their weekends either.

Karen heard voices raised in greeting as the latter arrived. This meant she would soon be busy with her first patient. The knowledge came as a relief. No sense in thinking about Arlene and Raif. Nothing *to* think, really. Arlene's presence at Long Beach didn't change Karen's position in any way.

She got through the day easily enough, helped by a busy series of appointments that ended well after two without her succeeding in squeezing in lunch. Evening surgery began again at seven. When she emerged into the waiting-room, though, the place still looked crowded. Stephanie and Raif were both there, and two others as well. Arlene, dressed now in a top of matt black suede and leather, with matching trousers that tapered tightly to finish at her lower calves, and Glenn Thorne, holding a newly bandaged thumb.

'For you, Karen,' Raif said, pointing to Glenn, who stepped forward.

'I feel bad doing this,' he said. 'But Mom swore to me that you wouldn't mind.'

'I'm sure I won't,' Karen said, smiling. 'What is it?'

'I was helping in the garden and I cut my thumb on an old can. I had a tetanus shot several years ago, but I can't remember exactly when, and she insists I need a booster. I'm sure she's right.'

'It'll only take a minute,' Karen assured him.

'It was painful holding the steering-wheel on the way in,' Glenn said now. 'I'm afraid the cut will stiffen up— it's right at the base of the thumb—and I'll have to ask you to drive us up to Mount St Helens on Sunday.'

'Perhaps I should take a look at the cut as well, then,' Karen decided.

But Arlene's attention had been drawn by the reference to Mount St Helens.

'Raif? Mount St Helens! We've never been. At least, I haven't. Would you take me on Saturday?'

'Sure,' Raiford agreed, with apparent ease.

Karen bit her lip suddenly. It was hard, in spite of all her resolutions, to hear the two of them calmly making plans like this, with the easy assumption that of course they would spend the day together. Now, it appeared, they were going for a walk along the beach before eating an early restaurant meal, just as he and Karen had done so recently.

Karen found herself wondering about Arlene's expensive outfit. The slightest splash of salt water on those trousers could easily ruin them with a permanent watermark. Raif dressed very casually on the beach, and somehow he didn't seem like a man who'd have all that much patience with a woman who kept yelping about her clothes and skittering out of reach of the water.

Oh, gracious heavens! What a bitchy thought! Arlene wanted to look nice for going out to dinner, and knew she wouldn't have time to change again.

'Come into the surgery,' Karen said to Glenn Thorne, and when they emerged again some minutes later the other three had left.

She half expected him to suggest coffee or a snack together now, but he didn't, just saying instead that he would see her for the film tomorrow night, then driving off in his ordinary green car, after an absent. 'Goodbye.'

Karen didn't blame him. He was really suffering over the woman who had left him, and didn't have much room inside himself at the moment for doing anything except conquering that pain. She had no illusions that this could be the beginning of a romance between the two of them. It would be months, and maybe longer, before Glenn Thorne would be ready to love again. That suited Karen very well. She wasn't ready for anything herself, when only a few weeks ago she'd been waiting so eagerly for Raif.

A movie would be a good distraction, and she was looking forward to Sunday's outing purely as a tourist. Thank goodness, though, that Arlene and Raif had decided to make their trip on Saturday!

CHAPTER NINE

'WE WERE living in Portland during the time of the eruption,' Glenn Thorne said, lighting a cigarette with the hand he had injured on Thursday. Karen's careful attention, and instructions about follow-up care, had made it painless enough for him to drive after all. Rosalie said he was smoking more than he used to since the break-up with Sharon, though.

Karen twisted to face him in the bucket-seat of his compact lime-green car. They had been driving for some time, talking casually at intervals as they gained altitude, and were now within sight of the high range of the Cascade Mountains, with their telltale volcanic shapes. It was a magnificent day, sunny, but with tangy cool air blowing through the open car windows, bringing just the faintest first hint of autumn scents with it.

Karen's memory of the dramatic eruption of Mount St Helens in May 1980 was only a hazy one. That was ten years ago now. She had been a medical student back then, in the early part of her course, too busy with study in London to do more than scan newspaper and television news coverage at irregular intervals. She remembered one headline and a grainy picture, but that was all, and really she had no idea what she would be seeing today.

'Were you frightened?' she asked Glenn.

'I was nineteen.' He smiled briefly. 'If I was scared, I didn't admit it, even to myself. I was playing baseball that morning. We'd gotten to the field early for some practice before the game, and we'd just started to pitch each other a few balls when. . .hardly any sound. It was very strange. Apparently people heard it very loudly hundreds of miles away. But an enormous billow of ash and cloud. Like a nuclear bomb, I suppose. The whole side of the mountain just blew away, and it's over thirteen hundred feet shorter now. The ash went mainly eastward, but we got our share of it. Later, of course. At the time, we all just stopped what we were doing and stood there, mouths hanging open, I guess. We couldn't believe it. We raced around. The whole town raced around yelling at each other and telling each other what they'd seen. No one listened to anyone else. There was fear and sadness later on. People died. And the Columbia River was nearly choked with ash and mud. It felt for a while as if we were living in a geology lesson. Or maybe the end of the world.'

Karen laughed, fascinated by the account. A volcano did seem strangely out of place in the modern world, particularly in a country like the United States, where nature seemed so dominated by humanity, so heavily under harness.

They stopped for petrol at that point, and Glenn lapsed into silence again, breaking it only to mutter a mild oath when the car had trouble starting after the tank was filled.

'Visitors' Centre first?' he asked as they came to a sign indicating a road that led off the main highway.

'Yes, please,' Karen answered. 'So I know about what I'm seeing.'

The Visitors' Centre had only been open for a few years, and was an airy modern building, typical of the well-presented displays in American national parks and museums.

'That's your partner's car, isn't it?' Glenn said as they entered the centre. He was pointing to a dark blue tank-like vehicle, half hidden now behind a camper van.

Karen shrugged. 'I don't think so. He said on Friday

they were going to come here yesterday,' she answered with a pretence at being casual.

Raif *had* said so, last thing on Friday afternoon. She had noted it specially, having been afraid he and Arlene might have had a change of plan. Anyway, there were plenty of cars on the road the same as or similar to his.

A film presentation was just about to begin as they reached the first display. 'Want to see it first, and then look at the rest?' Glenn asked, and Karen nodded.

She found the mixture of still and moving images, and the clear commentary, interesting and also strangely moving. Displays of human foolishness and courage, of scientific knowledge, and of nature's casual yet noble power, came through the short presentation, and, when Karen left the theatrette, she had to quickly wipe away some tears brought forth by the sheer savage beauty and drama of it all, a reaction which she knew most people would think foolish. Getting teary over a volcano!

They began to study the displays, which showed avalanches and mud-slides, lava formation and tree devastation, then Glenn excused himself. 'Do you mind if I go outside for a cigarette?'

'Not at all,' Karen said. 'You've seen all this before, haven't you?'

'Yes, I brought Sharon up here two years ago,' he said heavily, and she cursed herself for leading him into the statement.

She wondered if the day had stuck strongly in his memory, and if part of his reason for bringing her here today was to deal with the ghosts of the past somehow. No doubt Sharon would be on his mind as he stood outside with that cigarette. . .

Still, Karen didn't mind in the least having to study the displays by herself. It was as she emerged from the walk-in model of the interior of the volcano that she heard the two familiar voices. Raif and Arlene. It *had* been his car.

They were standing just opposite, with their backs towards her, studying some of the photographs of the mountain both before and after the explosion. Raif wore casual pale demin jeans and a shirt of red and black check, and Arlene was dressed again in her black trousers and top.

'I want to come up here some time for several days at a stretch and paint it all,' Raif was saying. Arlene gave a snort.

'More of your pretty little landscapes?' she said, with a light tone that carried a snide ring. It was an inaccurate comment too, Karen thought. Raif's paintings had a power that wasn't covered by the adjectives 'pretty' and 'little'.

'Well, I doubt that these ones will all be pretty,' Raif answered Arlene, carefully smooth.

'I don't know why you keep on with it, Raiford, I really don't,' Arlene said, intensely now, her Californian accent strong. 'What's the point? You never study the art scene in important places like LA and New York. The kind of things you do aren't selling now. The good galleries want work that says something about the urban world, that shocks and provokes. Landscapes have been around since the year dot. You've got to see how art is evolving and follow that trend or you're wasting your time. You *are* wasting it! I've told you——'

'Yes, you *have* told me,' Raif broke in. 'You've convinced me no one would buy my work and no gallery would ever take it, so I don't try. I paint as I want to paint, and that's all I'm interested in doing now.'

'But you're talented, Raif!' Arlene wailed desperately. 'You could make big money and be the toast of the town if you'd just. . .'

'If I'd copy what a few other trendy types are doing?' Raif queried cynically.

'Not copy,' she answered primly. 'Take further. Push the boundaries of——'

'I'm a doctor,' Raif said, cutting off her words. 'I paint for myself, not to try to please critics or get into some scene I know nothing about.'

'And I'm trying to get you to. . .'

'Excuse me, please.' An older woman stood behind Karen, tapping on her shoulder, and she realised shamefully that she had been blocking the tunnel-like exit of the model.

She had felt stranded by Raif and Arlene's presence, afraid to go past them in case they caught sight of her, but of course she had to move now. In any case, she had no right to listen to their conversation. If she wasn't prepared to declare her presence, then she should move away.

They didn't seem to notice Karen as she passed them, and she caught Raif's low angry tones briefly again. 'Don't try to change me into what you want me to be, Arlene—the way you change your patients, give them the nose or the breasts or the chin they used to have, or that they've always wanted.'

Then once more she was out of range.

Lovers quarrelling in a public place never sounded pleasant, but an outsider couldn't know what lay behind the angry words. Karen tried to put what she had overheard out of her mind, and was relieved to see Glenn making his way towards her again, his clothing smelling strongly of cigarette smoke, but his face a little more relaxed.

They paused over the next exhibit, concerned with the re-growth of plant and animal life on the devastated lower slopes of the mountain, and then Karen heard Arlene's voice rising above the general level of sound and voices nearby. She was one of those people with the confidence not to care if they were overheard in public.

'Why didn't they just drop a bomb on it, to bring on the eruption? That way they could have completely evacuated the area and no lives would have been lost.'

'Like inducing labour so women don't give birth on holidays and weekends?' Raif queried cynically.

'Hey, it *is* your partner,' Glenn said, turning at the sound of his voice.

'Oh, so it is,' Karen murmured, her heart sinking. Still, the meeting was probably inevitable. She followed Glenn as he stepped closer to Raif and caught his attention.

'Hello, Dr Calvert,' Glenn said as Raif recognised him and smiled.

'I'd forgotten you were planning this trip too,' the doctor said blandly, without any nuance of welcome.

'I thought you were coming yesterday.' As accusing tone crept into Karen's voice, which she failed to control.

'We got up too late,' Arlene put in. She was eyeing the newcomers without interest. 'Raiford. . .?'

But he interrupted. 'Arlene thinks the experts should have tried to control the eruption with explosives.'

'Lives might have been saved,' the square-faced blonde argued defensively, her small nose tilted indignantly. Karen thought of Raif's comment about noses and chins. Arlene was a plastic surgeon, it seemed. Was her own bland little nose the product of a fellow surgeon's skill with a knife? Karen had never thought much about *her* nose. It was very straight, tilting neither up nor down, perhaps a little *too* straight, and more prominent than a Hollywood plastic surgeon would have considered proper, but it seemed to dwell very contentedly on her face. She'd had it all her life, and couldn't imagine a change.

'And other lives might have been lost instead,' Raif

was answering Arlene. 'I just don't think everything in the world can be made tame. I wouldn't *want* a totally tame world.'

'It's not possible,' Glenn said.

'From what I've seen here,' Karen put in tentatively, forgetting about noses, 'people were given a worthwhile reminder of that. And for me—admittedly, I'm not someone who lost anything through the eruption—it's been a reminder of how beautiful the savagery of nature can be.'

'Have you had enough, Raif?' Arlene asked in a sweet, purring voice. 'You've been here before, and I don't want to bore you. Let's leave—er—Dr Madigan and her friend to themselves and find somewhere for our picnic, shall we?'

'If you like,' Raif agreed casually, but Karen thought that he was still masking some anger and a desire to resolve this second argument about the volcano. Some couples were always arguing. It was part of the essential fabric of their relationship, and they were happy with it. Somehow, Karen wouldn't have thought that Raif would want that kind of thing himself.

'I think we're about ready to leave, ourselves,' Glenn said. 'Karen wants to get a better view of the mountain itself, as well as the mud-slide area, and that doesn't give us much time.'

So it ended up that the four of them left the Visitors' Centre together.

'After that display, you'll probably be disappointed that we can't get closer,' Glenn said when they separated from the other two after brief goodbyes, and climbed into the lime-green car. 'The summit is still considered dangerous, and anyway, it's a long hike. There are some walking trails leading to the devastated area, but the roads were destroyed by the eruption, and they haven't rebuilt them——'

He broke off. He had just turned the key in the ignition and nothing had happened. He tried again. Still nothing. He sat for a moment and then spoke. 'It's the starter motor.'

'Oh.' Karen put her sketchy knowledge of car mechanics together with her reading of the exasperation in Glenn's voice and added it up to something serious.

'If we hurry——' her companion was already getting out of the car as he spoke '—we can catch your friends. . .'

Karen followed in the wake of his desperate sprint, cursing all mechanical things. 'Hey, Dr Calvert! Dr Calvert!' Glenn was calling.

The big old car was just turning out of the car park, but Karen saw Raif's elbow appear at the window and his dark head crane around. The car slowed, and Glenn caught up to it.

'You're not very good with cars, are you, Dr Madigan?' Raif said sternly as Karen arrived several moments later.

'I'm not?' Karen blurted, confused. Then she caught the teasing glint in his grey eyes and laughed. 'Oh. . . Your brakes. . .'

'And your getting bogged in the first place,' he reminded her with mock severity. 'Now this starter motor. Clearly, you send out some kind of force-field that's hostile to engine parts.'

In the passenger seat, Arlene shifted impatiently, and Karen decided once and for all that she didn't envy their relationship. That should have made her feel better about Raif, but unfortunately it didn't. The small teasing moment they had just shared had given her more pleasure than the entire three hours of Glenn Thorne's company, although Rosalie's son was a perfectly pleasant person and a very adequate tour companion.

'Any ideas,' Glenn?' Raif was saying now.

'Give it a push-start and head for the next garage, I suppose,' the younger man answered gloomily, rubbing his dark reddish hair into an untidy bush.

'That'll spoil your day.' It was addressed to Glenn, but Raif's glance strayed beyond him to where Karen was standing, and again he gave her a smile that left her weak with longing for him. 'Why don't you leave the car here and come with us for the afternoon? We'll stop here and collect it on our way back—it'll mean a bit of back-tracking, but not much. Then we'll push-start it, and, as long as you can get back to Long Beach without stalling the engine, you can take it to a garage there. . .'

'And save myself a lot of trouble, as well as saving Karen's day,' Glenn finished for him. 'That'd be great, Dr Calvert, it really would. Karen?'

'If you're sure you can fit us in. . .' was all Karen could say. Arlene nodded and smiled with apparent pleasure at the prospect of a foursome, but was it sincere? Doubtful.

It didn't take long for their things to be transferred from the lime-green car. Glenn had proposed buying lunch somewhere rather than taking a picnic, so they had no basket, although Karen had packed fruit, crackers, cheese, cake and a Thermos of tea on a last-minute impulse this morning.

'We thought we'd picnic at Yale Reservoir,' Raif said as he started his car again. There was plenty of room in the wide rear seat for both Karen and Glenn. 'It's a bit of a drive, but it's a lovely spot, and gives you a good clear view of Mount St Helens in the distance to the north. We could have gone up the old highway to the south fork of the Toutle River and looked at the remnants of the mud-slides, but those are far less spectacular now than they once were, and as you saw in the photos at the Visitors' Centre. Regeneration is softening the whole landscape remarkably quickly.'

'Raiford, darling, you're not a tour guide,' Arlene protested artificially.

He said nothing in reply, being busy merging on to the highway, and the tension remained hovering between them. Glenn stared moodily out of the window, perhaps reminded of scenes in his own recently ended relationship. Karen was silent too. At first her heart had leapt at the thought of spending the rest of the day with Raif, but now she was wishing it hadn't happened. It didn't seem as if anyone was going to enjoy it very much.

Once they had spread out a picnic rug on a grassy slope which gave good views of the jaggedly broken cone to the north, Karen's spirits improved. The mountain seemed to brood like a living presence, as if it might choose to become active again at any time. The higher slopes still showed patches of snow, but there was a wisp of smoke like a crooked halo above the summit. Was it just cloud, or was the lava dome growing in the middle of the desolate crater giving forth gases and ash today?

'Raif, you've done yourself proud, as usual,' Arlene said, lolling on a second rug and reaching her plate out for some pâté and crackers.

Karen was glad that she and Glenn had had at least something to provide, but it fell short of the generous offerings in Raif's basket. Arlene sat up lazily and began to eat. She had protested about the possibility of getting grass stains on her expensive suede and leather outfit before agreeing to the grassy site, and it was fortunate that Karen had thought to bring the rug from Glenn's car.

It was nicest just to watch the mountain as she ate, and to sit in silence while the other three chatted behind her. No, it was really Arlene who was talking, in a lively and quite entertaining manner, about people she and Raif both knew in the medical world in Los Angeles. Clearly, their relationship wasn't the recently begun thing Karen had assumed at first. It hurt, and should have angered her, that Raif had deceived her from the very beginning, but she was beyond anger now.

Glenn laughed, for the first time that day, at Arlene's anecdotes, and Raif had a number of questions to ask. They had almost finished the picnic meal when Arlene became occupied in commenting on something that Glenn had said, leaving Raif free to notice Karen's long silence.

'All right?' He shifted to face her, and his hand pressed against the side of her arm.

Quickly, and without replying to his quiet, laconic question, she jerked herself away from his touch and saw him glance down, surprised and frowning. He hadn't even realised that he had been pressing her skin, and Karen felt foolish with her prim physical response—like some obsessive old maid who saw shocking innuendo in everything.

'Yes, I'm fine,' she managed to say, too late. 'Just enjoying the view.'

'Yes, perhaps we should have saved our Los Angeles gossip for the trip home,' he said quietly. Arlene and Glenn were still talking. 'Silence is nicer. Words drown out our perceptions.'

'Do you always paint alone?' Karen asked, not stopping to think about whether it was a wise question after this morning's overheard exchange on the subject of his art.

'Yes, I do. Or I always have done, so far,' he said, beginning to close off as she had feared he would. 'If I ever found a companion who. . .no, never mind. As you said, silence is nicer. Why chat? I think I'll go for a walk. There's a better vantage-point further on.'

He sprang to his feet, his practical walking shoes a contrast to Arlene's frivolous gold sandals with their low but still spiky heels. It seemed odd that they hadn't consulted each other better about what to wear. Karen, in white leather pumps and floppy-topped white cotton socks below her cinnamon trousers and apricot blouse, had prepared for a walk today, but Raif was striding away without waiting for anyone, so it looked as if he intended to be alone.

She waited for a decent interval, murmured an excuse to the other two, then wandered off in a slightly different direction from the one Raif had taken. Arlene and Glenn were both lying on the rugs now, with the remnants of the food between them, subsiding into an afternoon doze.

At first, Karen thought she would keep walking along the road in search of a closer, clearer view of the mountain, but then the tangy scent of the pine woods beckoned and she decided to seek the hidden solitude of the trees. It was cool and very fragrant there, as drifts of deep cushiony needles and brittle twigs rustled or snapped under her neat comfortable pumps. Two tiny grey squirrels bounded away from her and up a tree trunk, their tails undulating with delicate, almost feathery softness.

She stopped to run her hands over the rough texture of the tree bark, lost in physical sensation, and heard birds calling from hidden branches. Some of them would be on their way south soon, as autumn advanced. She wasn't thinking about Raif at all. . .

And then he was there, startling her into a shocked gasp as she brushed past a thick-trunked old tree and found him leaning moodily against its other side. He turned instantly towards her, with a rasp of surprise in his throat that echoed her own instinctive sound.

He recovered himself and laughed. 'I must have been thinking too hard. I didn't see you!'

'And I didn't see you,' Karen responded. 'My heart dropped about ten feet.'

Her right arm was still trailed against the trunk of the tree and he was leaning against the bark, resting on his left elbow, so that they were standing quite close. It felt like a secret rendezvous here in the stillness of the forest, and when they spoke their voices naturally fell almost to a whisper.

'The other two aren't with you?' he said.

'No. When I left, they looked as if they were having a doze.'

A silence fell between them and Karen could hear her heart pumping the blood through her, and throbbing it in her ears. Her awareness of him caught her breath and made her throat tighten and her skin tingle. Going into his arms in response to the slow reach of his right hand pulling gently at her waist seemed the most natural thing in the world.

She buried her face in the warm curve of his neck, felt the softness of his flannel shirt, and drank in the scent of his maleness, mingled with the fruity, fertile smell of the forest. When he coaxed her to move her face so that he could reach her lips and part them with his own, she drifted into a warm tide of pleasure that for a long time drowned out anything else.

It felt so right. How could it be anything but right?

But it wasn't right. No matter what her body told her, this was forbidden. Arlene and Raif had an established relationship and Karen, his professional partner, was an interloper. Would Raif think she had come into the forest deliberately looking for him to try and steal this secret moment of passion? Perhaps subconsciously she had. . . Or perhaps he had seen her coming, had hidden ready to create a meeting and give himself the pleasure of a clandestine encounter.

Whichever was the truth, it was sordid and went against what she believed. Surely it went against what Raif had always claimed too—that he was open about what he wanted, and that he didn't believe in playing games. It was this thought that finally gave her the strength to resist her own feelings and his mounting demands.

With one last surge of pleasure, she felt the hard press of his thighs and hips against her, and then with a movement that was almost snake-like in its suppleness and speed, she had twisted away from him and was facing him at a distance of several yards.

'I'm angry, Raif,' she said, in a voice that vibrated with feeling.

'Arlene and I are finished, Karen——' be began, but broke off at her shout of cynical laughter.

'That's a line a lot of women must have heard down the ages,' she said. 'Have you told her that yet, or am I the first to know?'

'No, I haven't "told her",' he growled, staring down and rasping his hand against the rough bark of the tree beside which he still stood. 'It's not something people. . . At least. . .'

'I don't want to hear your justifications,' Karen burst out, then she plunged on, not caring how much of herself she was giving away. 'When I thought you were free, I wanted this. That was quite clear, wasn't it? Too clear, I suppose.'

'No, that's not——'

She refused to let him finish. 'But I'm not a woman who falls for those kind of lines—"our relationship is empty". "I'm going to tell her tonight". "When I met you, I knew everything I thought I had with her was false".' Her mimicry was harsh and accurate, and she saw him flinch. 'I'm not interested in the kind of man who can go straight from one woman to the next, overnight. What kind of trust does that create for the future? None! I'm going now, Raif. I'm going to walk through these woods by myself for half an hour, I don't want you to follow, and I don't want to hear any more of those old lines from you. If you want to know, they *hurt*!'

Her voice broke and she stumbled away from him, blinded for some moments by tears that filled her eyes again as fast as she could blink them away. As soon as she could see well enough, and could control the shaking in her limbs, she broke into a run, thankful for the spongy soles of her shoes and for the thick carpet of needles underfoot that reduced the noise of her erratic footsteps to dull thuds and swishes.

She was breathless and damp by the time she stopped, and when she looked back the trees had closed in behind her and Raif was thoroughly out of sight. She made a quarter turn, and the trees looked the same. She revolved completely on the spot, and again in every direction the trees stretched, darkening and closing in in the distance and offering no clue as to where she ought to go. . .

On the edge of panic, Karen willed herself to regain control. First she bent over and rested her hands on her knees, breathing deeply until her panting slowed and stilled, then she took out a handkerchief and wiped away the beads of sweat from her forehead. Mosquitoes began to gather, lured out of the damp carpet of needles by the hot scent of her body.

Once more she looked back in what she thought was the direction of their picnic spot, hoping to see a glimmer of open grassy field through the trees, or, yes, hoping to see Raif coming after her. It was pitiable and pathetic! Even after that naked scene, she wanted him to rescue her! It was like asking to be treated as a child, to have her tantrum ignored and to have an adult in the background waiting to pick up the pieces.

Well, Raiford Calvert was nowhere to be seen, and she felt a fleeting instant of warmth for him. He respected her enough to take her demand for solitude seriously, and it was time she respected herself that much—no, *more* than that. She started to look around carefully and realised that she was standing on a significant slope. Had she been running uphill? Downhill? No, the terrain she had covered was flat, so she must have been traversing this hillside at the same height.

This gave her the clue she needed to retrace her steps, and she turned and began to walk slowly back, breathing steadily and letting coolness seep once more into her cheeks. The slope flattened out, the trees in the distance opened out a little, and she thought she recognised the place where she and Raif had come across each other.

Wrong. When she finally emerged from the pine trees, she saw that she had come out several hundred yards away from the point where she had entered them. Those trees were deceptive. Still, no harm was done. She could see the other three in the distance, their activity becoming clearer as she approached.

Arlene had a heavy camera around her neck and was taking some pictures of the mountain, with Raif posing casually for her in the foreground. Glenn was folding up his picnic rug as he walked towards Raif's car. He was the first one to catch sight of Karen.

'Here she is!' he called to the other two, as if they had been getting anxious about her, and Raif shifted his gaze immediately, so that Arlene gave an impatient cry.

'You've spoiled that one, Raif. You'll just be a blur!'

Raiford ignored her, left his pose and strode towards Karen, who had bent down to pick up the other rug and fold it. 'We were about to send out a search party,' he said.

His light comment masked a concern that made Karen flush. She concentrated on neatening the corners of the rug. 'I wasn't lost,' she answered in the same light tone he had used.

It would have been easier to hear anger in his voice. It

disarmed her own hostility towards him to find that he wasn't going to lash out at her, after those home truths she had delivered across the soughing silence of the pines. There was an integrity in him which came out and caught her just as she was determined to find a murky motivation behind everything he said and did.

'We should be heading back, then,' he was saying now. 'By the time we make the detour to your car, Glenn, and get it going again. . .'

'I know.' Glenn nodded. 'I told my parents I'd be in for a meal. You're invited too, Karen.'

'Do you two live together?' Arlene asked, having approached, camera case banging against her waist, in time to hear Glenn's words. Her heavily made up eyes had narrowed a little, perhaps because she was slightly out of breath.

Karen saw Glenn's face twist at the reminder of his recent break-up, and stepped in hastily.

'Heavens, no,' she said. 'I'm more a friend of Glenn's parents. He's staying with them for a week or so, and when he heard I hadn't seen Mount St Helens, he very nicely offered to make a day of it, that's all.'

Arlene nodded, clearly wondering about the two medical partners and how well they got on together after hours. Had she detected something in Raiford's manner when he emerged from the pine woods, or was Karen behaving differently somehow? Or was she the kind of woman who would be suspicious merely because Raif and Karen had both been alone in that concealing maze of pines at the same time?

Well, her suspicions had been justified, hadn't they? Karen thought bitterly. One moment of nearness to Raif, and her principles had crumbled. She was no better than he was. Thank heavens she'd had the courage at least to push that angry scene through to the end. Would it be enough to protect her from her own helpless response to him?

With a sinking heart, Karen knew that the answer was no, and, as the four of them drove in silence back to the Visitors' Centre, she found the only solution staring her in the face. She had entered into partnership with him unwillingly. Perhaps it had been doomed from the beginning. In any case, the only thing to do now was to dissolve it.

CHAPTER TEN

'It's been hard to get to talk to you alone,' said Arlene Decker, in a breathless, apologetic tone as she stood on Karen's front doorstep, silhouetted against the fading dusk.

'Talk to me alone?' Karen echoed thinly.

She clutched a full-sleeved fluffy black angora cardigan-jacket more closely around her as a draught swept through the open doorway. The smoky green linen dress that hugged her slim shape was no longer warm enough in this early autumn weather, and the delightfully soft black angora was a new purchase.

Arlene wore black too. It appeared to be her usual colour—tonight in the form of a lacy strapless dress that lifted and stiffly cupped the perfect circular globes of her full breasts, and was topped by an asymmetrically draped jacket of soft and very expensive suede, spoiled, in Karen's opinion, by a lavish encrusting of beading and sequins. She stood back and gestured into the tiny hallway. Clearly Arlene wanted to be invited in.

'I'm on my way to pick up a take-out pizza in Klipsan Beach,' she said. 'Raif's gorgeous cooking is all very well, but sometimes it's just too much darned trouble dabbling in a kitchen.'

Karen remembered the warm, relaxed feeling she had had the night she and Raif had started to make that pasta meal that never got eaten. She had enjoyed dabbling round in a kitchen with him, actually. And wasn't strapless black a little overdone for eating pizza out of a cardboard box?

She shut off this nasty train of thought. She had no

justifiable reason to dislike Arlene, even if she didn't particularly care for her style. Arlene was speaking.

'Could I beg you for a drink?' she coaxed, sitting on Karen's modest grey fabric-covered couch.

'Of course.' What kind of scene was Arlene preparing for?

'Bourbon and Coke?'

'I'm afraid all I have is sherry, wine or fruit juice. Oh, and some beer,' Karen added, remembering that she kept a six-pack in the fridge these days for Geoff Thorne, when he and Rosalie dropped over.

'I'll take white wine and orange juice, then,' Arlene said, and Karen went to the kitchen to turn off a home-made soup that was boiling on the stove ready for her evening meal, before making the drinks. Although she wasn't particularly thirsty herself, it seemed easiest to keep Arlene company with the same thing.

'I've come to ask a favour of you,' Arlene said, leaning forward and gulping at her drink with a lack of grace that detracted from the high-fashion elegance of her expensive clothes.

'A favour?' Why was it that Karen could only echo Arlene's last words with a blank intonation? She made herself sit back and relax in the armchair opposite Arlene's couch, dangling one slim hand over the edge of the armrest and holding her misty glass with the other.

'Raif is interested in returning to Los Angeles, but he's concerned about the partnership. You've probably realised by now he has scruples about that sort of thing. I'm asking you to make it clear to him that you won't mind if he leaves.'

Karen couldn't find an answer. The suddenness of the request and the bluntness of Arlene's wording had taken her completely by surprise. But the cosmetic surgeon misinterpreted the hesitation.

'Of course, I'd give you some financial incentive. . .'

'You mean a bribe?' Karen breathed, incredulous.

'My God, what an awful word!' Arlene exclaimed. 'No, I simply mean some compensation for any monetary setback you might incur through the change.'

'But why should it be you that pays this... compensation?' asked Karen. 'Surely Raif——'

'I don't want Raif to feel he's asking for favours,' Arlene interrupted. 'Perhaps I'm being over-sensitive.'

That wasn't the word, Karen thought. Insincere, more likely. A game was being played here, but she didn't quite know what it was.

'Would you be very unhappy if Raif left?' Arlene was asking now.

'My feelings wouldn't enter into it,' Karen said smoothly, sensing that at least part of Arlene's intention during this chat was to probe at Karen's attitude to her partner. 'If Raiford's plans change and he doesn't want to stay in Long Beach, I'll have to find a new partner, or continue on my own. I'm sure he and I can come to some arrangement openly and honestly.'

'Of course,' Arlene said hastily. 'I'm purely concerned about the possibility of Raif making a sacrifice that's completely unnecessary. Just make it clear to him that you won't feel hard done by, that's all I'm asking, and I'm proving I'll see to it that you're *not* hard done by.'

Karen smiled and nodded. It sounded reasonable when worded so smoothly, but there was more here than met the eye, she was still convinced. 'And what is Raiford intending to do in Los Angeles?' she asked.

'He's always been interested in my specialty,' said Arlene. 'Cosmetic surgery. A few years ago he went through a career crisis and decided to drop out and think for a while. He had some idea that was he was going to combine general practice with painting, but he's realised that's naïve. He's really a very ambitious man, and now he's ready to return to his original goals. I think my little boy is finally growing up!'

'I'm sure you're pleased,' Karen said carefully.

She disliked the habit some women had of talking to another woman about a man as if he were a child. Raiford Calvert, for example, had always struck her as one of the most mature men she had ever encountered!

Arlene had drained her glass, and was standing now—again a movement that contained less natural grace than one might have expected from a woman with her level of outward glamour. She placed the empty glass on the wooden coffee-table in front of her, then picked up the smoky sea-green sphere that was Karen's beloved glass fishing float.

'Raif seems to have about fifteen of these wretched things,' she said, one long red nail making a raucous scratching sound on the surface of the glass.

'You don't like them?'

'They look like the sort of décor you'd find in a family fish restaurant called Jolly Jack Tar's, or something.'

Karen laughed. Arlene had a spiky but entertaining sense of humour. 'Well, I think it depends on the rest of the décor,' she said, in defence of her favourite possession. 'If you surround them with draped nets and plastic models of fish, yes, but if you just treat them as balls of glass and pile them on to an interesting surface. . .'

'Oh, I didn't mean to insult your interior decorating,' Arlene put in hastily.

'I was defending Raiford's, actually,' Karen answered, then her words broke off and she gasped as the ball slipped from Arlene's fingers and fell to the floor, eluding the futile grabs the glamorous surgeon made with her brittle-tipped fingers.

For a heart-stopping moment, Karen watched it bounce on Rosalie's rug, then it rolled harmlessly to a position near Arlene's feet, where she could bend down and retrieve it.

'Thank goodness for that!' she said, replacing it on the coffee-table in its shallow bowl.

'I hope you didn't break a nail or anything,' Karen said politely.

'These things? Oh, they're pretty indestructible. It's a shame I have to have them taken off before I start work on Wednesday.'

It was now Monday night. 'So you're flying back to Los Angeles tomorrow?' asked Karen.

'Yes. I'm leaving here first thing in the morning,' Arlene said brightly.

'And Raif?'

'I'm sorry?' The bottle-blonde frowned.

'When does Raiford think he'll be making the move? He must have a lot of settling up to do here, with the house. . .'

'Oh, it's not decided exactly,' Arlene said a little clumsily. 'As you say, there's a lot to do. . . And I'd better get on with it and pick up that pizza. Raif will give me a grilling. He won't believe my story about their getting our order wrong. . .'

'Oh, I don't think Raiford easily suspects other people of lying,' Karen said deliberately. 'When he's such an honest man himself.'

She felt petty a moment later, and didn't have any sense of triumph when she saw from Arlene's sudden flush that the shot had gone home. She ought to have maintained her dignity and kept herself untainted by those double-edged sallies that were thought of as women's traditional weapons between each other.

Weapons? she thought sadly as she shut the door after some polite goodnights and good wishes had passed between them. What battle was she fighting? She'd lost Raiford Calvert. No, she'd never had him. Those kisses they had exchanged and the time they had spent together only marked difficult times in Raif's relationship with Arlene. It was a classic situation.

Arlene's request tonight was ironic, really. Very timely. Karen had spent the day wondering whether to sell the practice outright and buy another one elsewhere, or whether to lease it to Raif and return to England to take a salaried hospital position. Selling it was now the obvious choice. It would release Raif, and it would release Karen herself from her memories of this tooshort summer in Long Beach. The region would forever remember her as fickle, selling up so soon after arriving, but it couldn't be helped.

As if to confirm her fear that she would become the subject of gossip once she put the practice up for sale, Karen's first patient the next morning was Dulcie Barnett, the woman Raif had warned her about two weeks ago, when she had made that mistake over Mrs Tanguy's prescription.

Karen had arrived early at work and hidden herself away immediately in her surgery, not feeling capable of exchanging casual cheery words with Raif this morning. She heard his voice in the waiting-room just as Dulcie was ushered in, and had to will herself to concentrate on the difficult old woman's long list of complaints. Mrs Barnett seemed to find it hard to concentrate on the list herself, and strayed off into the chatter that was her chief pleasure in life these days.

'I went down to Dr Rebbeck last time, for my arthritis,' she said. 'But this time I thought I'd try you. I don't like that Miss Stenlow of his. Never have, even when she was here with Dr Thomas.'

Karen smiled in a noncommittal way, knowing that when speaking to Barbara Stenlow Dulcie Barnett might well have claimed not to like Stephanie Zeigler—or Karen herself, for that matter.

'It's nice what you've got here now with Dr Calvert, isn't it?' Mrs Barnett went on. 'The two of you?'

'Yes, I'm enjoying the work very much,' Karen agreed carefully. Dulcie wanted a clue as to whether she and Raif were involved, but she wasn't going to get one. 'And, speaking of the work, you were wondering if we could change the blood-pressure medication you're taking at the moment. . .'

Mrs Barnett looked disappointed at having failed to find anything out, but did keep to the subject of her own health for the rest of the appointment.

Stephanie had gone to pick up lunch when Karen emerged from the surgery at half-past twelve, and Raif was sitting lazily on the reception desk, with one leg, clad in pale grey trousers, swinging back and forth. He seemed to be reading the appointment book, but looked up and smiled as Karen entered the room, and she felt her heart turn over as usual.

'So Arlene went back this morning,' she said brightly.

'Last night, actually,' Raif answered neutrally.

'Oh. . .' Karen was surprised. Arlene had definitely spoken of leaving this morning. 'I thought. . .'

'Her flight left from Portland, so she drove there last night and stayed at a hotel,' Raif elaborated.

'I see. . . I expect you're already making plans for a weekend down in Los Angeles,' she ploughed on firmly.

'Stop this chit-chat, please, Karen. I can't stand it.' The blunt command brought her up short, but he showed no mercy. 'If we can't say what's really on our minds—and I don't think we can at the moment—then let's not talk at all! Agreed?'

'What do you want me to do, Raif?' she asked helplessly. Arlene must have let slip that Karen had agreed to dissolve the partnership. Was that what he meant by 'what's really on our minds'?

'Don't do anything,' he said. 'I'm going for a walk. I'll have lunch in my office when I get back.'

He closed the appointment book with a snap and strode from the waiting-room, grabbing a black raincoat off the peg behind his door, then leaving the building with an abrupt crash of the door.

Karen let out the breath she had been holding and turned helplessly to the magazine rack, ploughing through several articles along the lines of 'Do you really know your man?' 'Seven ways to keep the pounds off this winter' and 'David Keyes—What is he *really* like?' without absorbing one word of their contents. She bolted down the turkey and salad sandwich Stephanie had brought her, then couldn't even look at the thick wedge of spicy-iced carrot cake. She took it into her office after some apologetic words to the blonde receptionist, and ate it there two hours later between patients, with a cup of tea.

Something has to happen, she thought, two weeks after this. I can't go on existing in this kind of limbo.

Autumn had definitely arrived—'fall' as it was called in America. Here, it *was* a fall too—an unceasing shower of brilliantly dying leaves. It was like the spread of a fire through the forest. Each day, new trees would colour themselves orange, crimson, golden brown, or rich buttery yellow, before baring their branches to form a carpet below, with the cool, unchanging green of firs and pines as a contrast.

Karen drove herself to Seattle for an extended weekend of city pleasures. A friend from England, Jennifer, married now to a diplomat, had written to say she would be passing through on a roundabout trip to Hong Kong, and could they meet? It had been fun to catch up on the news from home—was it home? Karen really wasn't sure—and to hear some of Jennifer's rather acid stories of life on the British diplomatic circuit.

On the way home, Karen had risked an accident several times as she craned her head in every direction, taking in the rapidly changing hues of the landscape. If she returned to England soon, with its more civilised vistas, would she miss the drama of all this? She thought that she would—the deep lakes and bays, the high, craggy mountains, the unbroken acres of forest, and the long, windswept stretch of beach with which she was so familiar now, in all its summer moods.

Yes, she would feel sad if she didn't get the chance to experience that beach in the fury of its winter storms as well. Why had Raif said nothing about the future? 'Let's not talk at all!' he had demanded, and she had taken him at his word, thinking that he would have to be the one to break their silence, since he was the one who had wanted it.

Oh, of course they talked a little. Greetings and goodbyes, the necessary discussion between one medical partner and another about patients and policy, new medications and problem diagnoses. But Arlene Decker wasn't mentioned, nor a single word about the possibility of Raif's leaving and going to Los Angeles.

It was blustery this afternoon. Karen had driven straight home after work and had flung herself down to the beach after changing into charcoal-grey wool trousers, an ivory mohair pullover and her rust-red jacket. The days were closing in. It was the middle of September already, and if she didn't go for a walk straight away it would be too dark and cold to go at all.

She turned south, feeling the westerly sting tears into her eyes. If Raif still walked frequently on the beach, she didn't want to encounter him, and he usually kept to the more northerly end. It was ridiculous to be thinking about whether she would encounter one man on fifteen miles of beach, but still. . .no sense in taking the risk.

The walk was unsatisfying today. The constantly changing shapes of billowy autumn cloud seemed to have lost their power to intrigue her, and actually, in spite of pullover and jacket, she was cold. Soon it would be the season of woolly hats and thick gloves, a long scarf, boots, and a heavy coat. Would winter in her little cottage be a chilly, desolate thing? Or would she have left Long Beach by then?

Suddenly she couldn't bear the uncertainty any longer, this limbo that left the future a hazy mist of different possibilities to which she had no chance to accustom herself. Perhaps Raif hadn't made up his mind about Los Angeles yet. Perhaps that strange visit of Arlene's was part of an attempt by her to force a final decision from him. Well, Karen needed a decision too, and she wasn't going to play games about it as Arlene had.

'When I want something, I go for it openly.' That was what Raif had said over two months ago when they'd been putting their medical partnership together.

'What's sauce for the gander is sauce for the goose, Raif,' Karen said aloud, her words carried away by a stinging blast of wind.

She turned on her heel, leaving the heavy, twisted imprint of her white leather pumps in the grey-yellow sand, and headed back towards the path through the sandhills that led to her cottage. She didn't change her clothing. Arlene had been overdressed in Karen's small house, with that too-voluptuous figure of hers that had very possibly been achieved with surgical help. To confront Raif, Karen wanted to be her natural self.

She freshened the day's light make-up, brushing deep brown mascara and a blended stroke of subtle greens to her eyelids to bring out the rich colour of her irises, and adding a glistening neutral lipstick, then she changed into soft leather boots that matched her rust-red jacket.

Instinctively, she knew that if she paused too long over this, she wouldn't do it, so just ten minutes after ending her walk she was starting the little red car and twisting the wheel to head down the street.

Oysterville was quiet as usual. Some gulls screamed and wheeled above the piles of oyster shell on the edge of the distant bay, and a boy passed whistling on a bicycle as he threw the local newspaper over fences and into gardens. It was nearly dark now, and he had only a couple of papers left.

Karen parked in the street outside Raif's house, closed the picket gate—she remembered how she had left it swinging that night when she had run away from him after his revelation about Arlene—then bent to avoid the brushing needles of a pine's low branch.

'Just a minute,' she heard Raif say to someone inside after she knocked at the green wooden door.

She would have undone the knock if she could. He wasn't alone. Horribly embarrassing! But when he opened the door a minute later, she saw he was on the phone. It stretched on a long cord in his left hand, and in the other he held a slim paintbrush, daubed with sea-green. He was wearing a rough and ready butcher's apron, smeared like an artist's palette with dozens of colours. He frowned at her and waved the brush. 'Come in.'

The door shut behind her and she went forward uncertainly into the lounge. It was chilly there, although a fire was laid in the grate, ready to be lit. Raif's voice continued in the background.

'Anyway, it's been a quiet summer, thank goodness. Yes, after all the drama of the *Star of Scandinavia*, I thought the coastguard and rescue service was in for a bad season.'

Karen guessed from the reference to the shipwreck that he was speaking to one of the coastguard people, and tried to shut her ears to the conversation. She didn't much like being reminded of the night the ship went down. Occasionally, it still brought with it that flash of sense-memory—herself in Raif's cold but sheltering arms as he stared down at her and said the word 'mermaid'.

She shivered. What had happened in Hans Andersen's fairy-tale? The mermaid had lost her prince to a mortal princess, and on their wedding night she had danced with feet that hurt like knives, then cast herself back into the sea, to mingle with the restless foam. Not a happy ending. She wondered if she should switch on the light. She decided to stay in darkness. It was dim and shadowy in here, but outside it was still bright enough to study Raif's garden through the windows and to see the occasional gull rising and dropping over the bay, as she waited in the room.

'OK, no trouble, Jim,' Raif was saying. 'I should have cleared up those questions for you at the time. Paperwork's a never-ending nightmare, isn't it?' He replaced the receiver and came into the sitting-room. 'What, standing here in the dark?'

'It's nice,' she said defensively, as he flicked a switch and made her blink and narrow her eyes. 'But I'm an interruption, and clearly I'm not the first one of the evening, so I'll go.'

'No, you won't, Karen.' It was very firm, and he was out of the room again and taking the stairs three at a time before she could think of another more forcefully polite exit line.

She heard his long strides echo on the wooden floor of his studio, and in a moment he was back again, apronless and empty-handed, with white shirt rolled to the elbows and a navy blue sleeveless pullover of soft, fine knit emphasising the squared strength of his shoulders.

'Now, you don't tend to drop in on me for social calls, so what is it?' He drew the curtains as he spoke.

'Don't say that as if it's my fault!' Karen retorted.

'Is that how I said it?' he queried lightly.

'Raif. . .!'

'All right.' He conceded the unfairness of his response.

'I need an answer from you.' She faced him, chin lifted in determination so that she looked taller than her slender five feet ten. 'Are you leaving. . .? Or *when* are you leaving Long Beach? Even if your plans aren't definite, it's unfair to leave me completely in the dark like this!'

'Who gave you the idea I was planning to leave at all?' he growled ominously, drawing his shoulders up tensely so that he seemed to hover over her in spite of her height.

'You. . . No, *you* didn't, you said you didn't want to talk at all,' she began, then amended, confused, 'Arlene said you wanted to go back to Los Angeles, and take up where you'd left off in cosmetic surgery four years ago.'

'When did she say this?'

'The night before she left. The night she drove to Portland.'

'She spent the evening with me. . .till nearly eleven, anyway. Did she pay you a midnight call?' His questions were wary, and there was a wall of emotion behind them that Karen could not read.

'No, she dropped in on her way to collect a take-out pizza,' she said, remembering too late that Arlene had been planning to fib about how long the pizza had taken to prepare. Still, why was she under any obligation to support Arlene's untrue story?

Raif was silent, staring at her for a moment, then turning to pace the room with his back to her, so that she could not even attempt to study his face. When he spoke, it was still with his back to her as he bent down to light the fire. His first match flickered and burnt out. Were his hands unsteady? Then the second match hissed into a yellow flame that was soon licking at the neat twists of newspaper and raw split lengths of kindling.

'Arlene and I have broken up,' he said slowly, watching the fire and quickly moving a fallen piece of wood. 'We never ate that pizza. It sat there in the kitchen getting cold and gluggy while we were in here talking. There seemed to be a surprising amount to say. . .'

'Yes, I gathered you'd been together for a long time,' Karen said carefully, standing very still in the room as she watched Raif. The first waves of warmth from the fire started to reach her as he sat back on his heels and collected some heavier wood from the cane basket on the hearth, ready to add it when the kindling and smaller logs started to burn down.

'We've known each other since we were teenagers,' he answered. 'As for being together. . . I think we split up three and a half years ago, when I first came up here.'

'That's an odd thing to say.' Karen laughed shortly.

'Why, Karen?'

'You just told me you'd broken up two weeks ago, and now you're saying over three years!'

'So it sounds like a contradiction? Do you think relationships are that simple?'

'The right ones are.'

He didn't reply. She couldn't resist the hypnotic glow of the fire any longer, and crept towards it, kneeling beside him on the rug and holding her hands out across the hearth.

'I was never well off as a child,' he told her. 'But Arlene and her family were downright poor. We both got through medicine on hard work and scholarships and night jobs, and we stood out from the other students like two sore thumbs. Arlene always swore she'd make up for it once she started practising. I never believed her, but she's kept her word and she's changed her style a lot. She used to be. . .well, much more like you. Casual, natural. These days she doesn't *own* a pair of flat shoes. . . Listen, you don't want to hear this sort of griping.'

'Not if you don't want to tell me,' Karen answered, fighting an awareness of his body beside her own.

'You're right—I *don't* want to. Not now. Not details. She's changed, that's all. So have I, but I've gone in a different direction. The last thing I'd ever consider is going back to Los Angeles, and into her surgical specialty. When I moved up here, we said we'd stay together on a long-distance basis. I realise now that both of us were assuming the other one would give way in a few months. I'd see that this was a boring backwater, or she'd be captivated by the beauty and wild rhythm of the seasons. I'd go back to fashionable, high-power medicine and try to make a name on the side in fashionable, high-power art, or she'd realise how superficial her lifestyle was compared with the reality of this.'

His gesture took in the house, the garden, all of Long Beach Peninsula.

'Of course it didn't work,' he went on. 'We only got further apart. I'm not even sure that she stayed physically faithful. I didn't ask. That's a bit out of character for me, as you might have guessed. I like things in the open. Perhaps I didn't want to know, or perhaps I just didn't care very much any more. In May, I went down there for four weeks, just after Will's death. She'd asked me to go. Things were. . .odd, awkward, and at the end of it she said she thought we ought to try a trial separation—horrible expression—and not see each other or even stay in contact, for six months. I agreed to it for her sake. I was sure it was the end, so when she rang a few weeks ago to say that the idea had been a mistake, I was very surprised, and it gave me a shock too. I'd been thinking of myself as a free man. . .free to make love to someone else. . .and here was this long-standing involvement creeping up on me again.'

He paused and poked at the fire with some brass-handled tongs, sending up a shower of crackling sparks.

'Karen, when she turned up here, I tried to make it clear from the beginning that we weren't together any more. She kept arguing. I didn't know how to make the final move. But, as I suspected, she'd had a brief, failed affair during our "separation", and she was clutching at straws. It wasn't really me she wanted. She slept in the spare room. I'm just glad, now, that we never got married.'

'You don't have to tell me all this, Raif,' Karen put in desperately.

He had said that his relationship with Arlene had come to an official end two weeks ago, and an emotional and physical end months before that, yet in these two weeks he had barely spoken to Karen. His fleeting need for her, like the affair that Arlene had been briefly involved in, was clearly gone now.

'No, I don't have to. . .' he was saying now. 'I said I'd be brief, didn't I? I'm a little surprised to find she told you that Monday night that I was moving to Los Angeles. She must have known it was out of the question, even before that last long talk we had.'

'Well, I'm glad you're staying, Raif,' Karen said, bright and matter-of-fact.

With a tremendous effort, she pulled herself to her feet, away from the lazy, living warmth of the fire that threatened to seduce her body into languorous relaxation. She went on speaking, more to drown out her feelings than for any other reason.

'I think we make good partners—medically, that is.'

'Only medically?' He had stood too, but lazily, and was only now uncurling to his full length in front of her, meeting her green eyes steadily with his own grey ones. Her heart began to beat slowly and heavily at his words.

'Only medically, my darling. . .?' he repeated, the endearment a whispered caress of warm air and soft lips against her ear.

His kiss came like a sweet juicy fruit, bitten into on a hot, thirst-filled day, and Karen hadn't known how parched she was from the lack of his touch until now. Her lips parted to explore his mouth, and she felt his hands slip beneath the bulk of her pullover and the silkiness of the blouse beneath to caress the elastic skin of her lower back.

'Why did you wait two weeks? Two whole weeks?' she murmured, closing her eyes so that it was only her senses of touch and taste that were drinking him in.

'Darling Karen,' Raif murmured against her hair. 'Don't you remember that day we went to Mount St Helens, when you nearly lost yourself in those pine woods?'

'Yes. . .?'

'You told me then that you had no respect for a man who went straight from one involvement to the next. It made absolute sense. I wanted to wait—I didn't know for how long, but when you came tonight. . . Is it still too soon? Too soon to ask you if you'll be my wife?'

She looked at him gravely, tilting her face upwards to meet his superior height.

'No, it's not too soon, Raif,' she said. 'I'd very much like to be your wife.'

'My wife and my partner, here together in this house.'

It was a long time before either of them spoke again. . .

'Karen. . .?' Raif rolled over lazily and put another

log on the fire, watching with pleasure as the flames flared up and glowed golden on her bare skin.

'Yes, Raiford?'

'Are you hungry?'

'Not yet.'

'Good, because I don't think we'll be ready to eat for a while, do you?'

'No...'

'And when we do eat, do you mind if it's only grilled cheese on toast?'

'I don't mind if it's dry crackers tonight, my darling,' she said.

OCTOBER 1990 HARDBACK TITLES

ROMANCE

Fragile Paradise *Jenny Arden*	3380	0 263 12573 4
A Summer Storm *Robyn Donald*	3381	0 263 12574 2
Man of Rock *Rachel Ford*	3382	0 263 12575 0
Time to Let Go *Alison Fraser*	3383	0 263 12576 9
Yesterday's Wedding *Kay Gregory*	3384	0 263 12577 7
The Wrong Kind of Man *R. Hammond*	3385	0 263 12578 5
The Gemini Bride *Sally Heywood*	3386	0 263 12579 3
A Bride for Strathallane *Stephanie Howard*	3387	0 263 12580 7
A Kind of Madness *Penny Jordan*	3388	0 263 12581 5
Lightning Strike *Marjorie Lewty*	3389	0 263 12582 3
Garden of Eden *Sandra Marton*	3390	0 263 12583 1
A Suitable Match *Betty Neels*	3391	0 263 12584 X
Lightning's Lady *Valerie Parv*	3392	0 263 12585 8
Counterfeit Marriage *Alexandra Scott*	3393	0 263 12586 6
Lovespell *Jennifer Taylor*	3394	0 263 12587 4
Sicilian Vengeance *Sara Wood*	3395	0 263 12588 2

MASQUERADE HISTORICAL ROMANCE

A Proud Alliance *Marion Carr*	M249	0 263 12729 X
A Marriage Made on Earth *Sheila Bishop*	M250	0 263 12730 3

MEDICAL ROMANCE

Unwilling Partners *Lilian Darcy*	D167	0 263 12723 0
Condition Critical *Judith Worthy*	D168	0 263 12724 9

LARGE PRINT

The Tiger's Lair *Helen Bianchin*	367	0 263 12415 0
Passionate Awakening *Diana Hamilton*	368	0 263 12416 9
Breaking Away *Penny Jordan*	369	0 263 12417 7
Spellbinding *Charlotte Lamb*	370	0 263 12418 5
It All Depends on Love *Roberta Leigh*	371	0 263 12419 3
The Girl With Green Eyes *Betty Neels*	372	0 263 12420 7
The Loving Touch *Catherine Spencer*	373	0 263 12421 5
The Golden Thief *Kate Walker*	374	0 263 12422 3

NOVEMBER 1990 HARDBACK TITLES

ROMANCE

Title	Author	No.	ISBN
Rancher's Bride	*Jeanne Allan*	3396	0 263 12601 3
A Vintage Affair	*Elizabeth Barnes*	3397	0 263 12602 1
The Stefanos Marriage	*Helen Bianchin*	3398	0 263 12603 X
Something From the Heart	*A. Browning*	3399	0 263 12604 8
Inherit Your Love	*Sally Cook*	3400	0 263 12605 6
Portrait of a Stranger	*Helena Dawson*	3401	0 263 12606 4
The Land of Maybe	*Sandra Field*	3402	0 263 12607 2
Mississippi Miss	*Emma Goldrick*	3403	0 263 12608 0
Jungle Lover	*Sally Heywood*	3404	0 263 12609 9
Wild Champagne	*Kate Kingston*	3405	0 263 12610 2
The Threat of Love	*Charlotte Lamb*	3406	0 263 12611 0
Flame of Avila	*Jean S. MacLeod*	3407	0 263 12612 9
No Reprieve	*Susan Napier*	3408	0 263 12613 7
Wild Heart	*Joanna Neil*	3409	0 263 12614 5
Not His Property	*Edwina Shore*	3410	0 263 12615 3
Endless Summer	*Angela Wells*	3411	0 263 12616 1

MASQUERADE HISTORICAL ROMANCE

Title	Author	No.	ISBN
Isabella	*Janet Grace*	M251	0 263 12731 1
A Passing Fancy	*Deborah Miles*	M252	0 263 12732 X

MEDICAL ROMANCE

Title	Author	No.	ISBN
Eastern Adventure	*Lisa Cooper*	D169	0 263 12725 7
Dangerous Practice	*Sheila Danton*	D170	0 263 12726 5

LARGE PRINT

Title	Author	No.	ISBN
One-Woman Crusade	*Emma Darcy*	375	0 263 12427 4
Silence Speaks for Love	*Emma Goldrick*	376	0 263 12428 2
Two Different Worlds	*Rosemary Hammond*	377	0 263 12429 0
Egyptian Nights	*Joanna Mansell*	378	0 263 12430 4
Night Fires	*Sandra Marton*	379	0 263 12431 2
Hidden Heart	*Jessica Steele*	380	0 263 12432 0
Intimate Deception	*Kay Thorpe*	381	0 263 12433 9
Stormy Surrender	*Patricia Wilson*	382	0 263 12434 7